Five Nights before the Summit

FIVE NIGHTS BEFORE THE SUMMIT

Mukuka Chipanta

WEAVER

PRESS

Published by Weaver Press, Box A1922, Avondale,
Harare, Zimbabwe. 2019

<www.weaverpresszimbabwe.com>

Typeset by Weaver Press
Cover Design: Baynham Goredema
Printed by Bidvest Printers, Cape Town

Distributed in Zambia by Gadsden Publishers, Lusaka.
Distributed in South Africa by Jacana Media.

ISBN: 978-1-77922-361-6p/back)
ISBN: 978-1-77922-362-3 (e-pub)
ISBN: 978-1-77922-363-0 (pdf)
ISBN: 978-9982-241199 (Gadsden Publishers)

Mukuka Chipanta is a Zambian aerospace engineer and author based in Maryland where he lives with his wife and daughter. *Five Nights Before the Summit* is Chipanta's second published novel. His debut novel, *A Casualty of Power*, published in 2016 by Weaver Press, received critical acclaim for its depiction of the cultural tensions between Chinese immigrants and the indigenous workers in the Zambian copper mines. The book was awarded Best First Book and Gold for General College Level Book at the 2017 Classic American Literary Awards in South Dakota, USA and longlisted for the 9Mobile (formerly Etisalat) award for African Literature in 2018.

Chipanta has an Engineering degree from the University of Manchester, UK as well as a Masters in Business Administration from the University of Connecticut, USA and the University of Hull, UK. He works as a manager of programmes in the aerospace industry to develop cutting edge technology for commercial and military aircraft. One of his proudest professional achievements is having played an integral role in designing the Boeing 787 Dreamliner.

Chipanta has contributed short stories to PM World, OZY Magazine and *Kalahari Review* and has had stories featured in several anthologies including *The Gods Who Send Us Gifts* – an anthology marking the 55th Anniversary of the famous Makerere Conference on African Literature, published in 2017. In 2019 Chipanta launched *Kutika! Modern African Stories*, a literary podcast showcasing a collection of his short stories in audio form.

A starving man will not notice a dirty plate.

Mary Renault

To banakulu Malaika.
Not a day goes by...

1

Trouble Brewing

2:11 a.m.

Twenty kilometres south of Lusaka ...

The darkness smothered Laura and Henry like a thick wet blanket. Laura had woken to the restless barking of Chanter and Whisky, her two boerboels. Sitting up in bed, she heard footsteps followed by poking at the windows. Getting out of bed, she peeped though the curtains, but could not see anything. She imagined men wielding crowbars, and was afraid.

Twenty years ago, the Hinckley couple had emigrated from England to settle in Northern Rhodesia, a serene British colony in the heartland of southern Africa. They had been much younger and filled with a sense of adventure. A few years later, after Zambia became independent, they had decided to remain, in stark contrast to many of their white contemporaries who fearing black majority rule had fled to Southern Rhodesia where whites still reigned supreme. Zambia had become home to Laura and Henry and they embraced the new nation with its lofty ideals of peace and inclusivity.

Laura involuntarily clenched her hands, feeling her nails sharp in her palms, as she sat down on the bed. Her heart was racing. She reached to clasp her husband's limp hand. He lay still. Henry had been wasted by a stroke several months previously. It had been unexpected at the comparatively young age of forty-six, but chain-smoking and a diurnal intake of whisky had doubtless done him in.

The affliction had left Henry virtually speechless and immobile along his left side. Laura, who had prematurely aged as a result, felt bitter and angry with God. How could 'HE' be so cruel as to transform a strong, curious man into a helpless, dribbling invalid?

Alert to every sound, Laura listened to the darkness. Henry grunted in discomfort – he could surely sense her fear.

"We'll be fine, my love," Laura whispered unconvincingly. "Just stay calm ... it'll be fine, you'll see." Once, not long ago, it would have been Henry offering words of reassurance but now the woman had to be strong for both of them. Suddenly, she heard two shrill yelps in quick succession, a whimper, and then silence. What had they done to Chanter and Whisky?

Beyond the bedroom walls, she recognised the sound of a door knob cycling furiously. Oh, if only they had a phone. She shut her eyes. It would have been useless anyway because the police would never come out so far at this late hour. A scream stuck in her throat. She clenched her teeth. Who would hear her? The homes of their farmhands were so far away that even if she shouted at the top of her voice, it would not carry the distance.

Henry's grunts grew louder, more desperate. Who was out there and what did they want? Money? Property? Or were they simply killers out for blood?

Laura stared into the darkness toward the wardrobe on the far side of the room. Their small padlocked safe was hidden underneath a removable panel inside the thick wooden base. It was a simple yet effective hiding place, difficult to find unless one knew where to look. It was where Laura kept the takings from the hatchery and the livestock pens, ready to be deposited into their bank account once a month by Elijah, their trusted driver and aide. However, that was not the only thing hidden in the safe. Laura's back stiffened as she remembered Henry's small sack of uncut emeralds that were worth a lot more than the takings from the farm. Then it dawned on her, could that be what the men outside were after?

Suddenly Laura heard a loud cracking sound which she could only imagine was the front door being prized open. Panic stricken, she let go of Henry's hand and stood up. Her hands shook and she took a long deep breath. Fear was in her mouth. She made a dash for the bedroom door and leaned her back against it. She knew it wouldn't make any real difference, the door could easily be kicked in, but what else could she do?

There was a sound of wood breaking followed by heavy footsteps and then falling objects – perhaps the flower vase had been knocked over or the ashtrays on the side tables had tumbled to the floor? One thing was certain, these were the steps and actions of determined men who felt little fear.

❄

3:14 a.m.

Lusaka – Kafue Road, a few kilometres east of Hinckley Farm...

Farai Muguru saw something looming in the distance, reduced the speed of his vehicle and turned down the volume on his AM radio. The sultry voice of Miriam Makeba was slowly supplanted by the mechanical purring of the engine. Adjusting his headlights to a full beam, he leant over the top of his steering wheel and squinted. There was a vehicle, a white station wagon, apparently lodged in a ditch on the side of the road. His foot weighed heavily on the brake pedal as he noticed the branch of a tree stretched across the tarmac. Farai blinked and trained his gaze on the area in front of him. A man was sprawled across the road – he was lying motionless on his back several feet from the stationary vehicle.

"*Hee-yah!*" Farai exclaimed as he brought his car to a complete stop and pressed the button to switch on his hazard lights. He checked the clock on his dashboard. It was 3:14 a.m. and there were no other vehicles in sight. Had it not been that he needed to visit his ailing brother in Kitwe, he would not have been on the road so late at night. Farai was one of many black men from Southern Rhodesia who had crossed the border to live and work in Zambia rather than suffer under Ian Smith's white minority government that treated

3

them as second-class citizens. He now lived and worked on one of the large commercial farms in Choma District several hours south of Lusaka. His brother, who had also fled Rhodesia, worked on the copper mines up north. Collapsing on one of his shifts complaining of nausea and vertigo, he had been rushed to hospital, where he fell into a coma. Now the doctors feared that he might not make it through the night. Hearing the news, Farai had borrowed a car from his boss, a white farmer, and set off immediately on the eleven-hour journey.

Farai's heart beat loudly. He hoped that the man lying on the ground was still alive. It looked as if the car had careered off the road because the driver was going too fast. Farai opened his door slowly. Leaving his engine running, he tentatively put a foot on the tarmac, straining his eyes to see into the darkness around him. He knew the stories – everyone did in Zambia – of traps being set by unscrupulous criminals. He knew he could lose his vehicle, if he left it. He felt a sense of foreboding but what choice did he have? There was a man on the tarmac apparently lying dead or badly hurt.

Farai took slow measured steps forward until he was standing a few feet from the victim. It was difficult to see but there appeared to be no visible signs of blood nor shattered glass as one might expect from a severe road traffic accident. He balled his fists in a final attempt to psych himself up to move closer still. Then, suddenly, he felt a sharp pain coursing through the back of his head. Before he knew it the sharp smell of asphalt filled his nostrils. He drifted like an untethered kite into a state of unconsciousness. The last thing he would remember seeing was a muddy pair of boots inches away from his face.

2

A Plan Gone Wrong

Amos Mushili gritted his teeth. Little had gone as planned, but being
a pragmatist, he believed that when confronted with a set of bad
choices, it's best to change direction. He had not planned to hurt the
white couple but that wretched little woman had proved more of a
problem than he'd anticipated. When he had pressed her to show
him where the safe was hidden and give him the key, she'd resisted.
He'd slapped her about, figuring this would do the trick, but he was
wrong. The small woman had fire within her. She'd snatched at his
balaclava and spat in his face. Then he'd lost it. He had laid into her
with his machete in a fit of rage. Before he knew it, there was blood
everywhere. After that, he had been left with no alternative but to
finish off her husband who was grunting feverishly on the bed. He
could not risk leaving a witness, even one that could neither walk nor
talk. Then, he had instructed his boys to search the entire house, they
would not leave until they had found what they had come for. Amos
was irritated, it should never have come to this – if only the woman
had done as she'd been told!

"*Ba* Amos, *yalayaka shani*, what are we going to do with him?"
Paul Mutamina, sitting in the passenger's seat, turned towards Amos
while Mambwe and Musa sat silently in the back seat of the small
Fiat. Amos did not respond.

Paul knew not to ask his leader the same question twice, so he
let it go and leant back in his seat. It was still dark and they were
approaching Lusaka. The plan, which Amos had initially spelled out,
was that they would gag and tie up the white couple, find and open

the safe, assuming that the whites had been frightened enough to give them the key, remove the bag, and then head northwards to a safe house on the Copperbelt, a six-hour drive away. There, they would lie low for a few days, and wait for things to cool off before making their next move.' This had been the plan, but now they had killed a person – two people, two white people – and the stakes were much higher. Amos knew that it was only a matter of time before the police would launch a manhunt. Soon uniformed men would stop and search every vehicle on the roads. As Amos looked ahead into the darkness, he knew that now more than ever he needed to find a different way out, if they were to survive the offensive that was sure to follow.

He turned down the volume on the radio. Paul, who was sitting next to him, perked up and turned to look at Mambwe and Musa in the back. The three men exchanged nervous glances. A few hundred feet ahead of them, were a set of striped bollards in the middle of the road. A police checkpoint!

"Ah, *ba* Amos, *yakakana* … *ba bugu*, there's a roadblock ahead!" Paul stated the obvious. Amos, who was never one to panic, said, "Just keep cool… let me do the talking." His voice was hard and clear. He slowed the car to a crawl. There were three men, two in police uniform and one in military fatigues with a gun slung across his shoulder. Amos cursed. There was no telling when and where these impromptu police checkpoints would spring up. Most simply existed to extort money from drivers.

Amos brought the car to a stop. The first policeman signalled for him to inch closer. Amos complied stopping a few feet in front of the second policeman and the soldier. Amos lowered his window. A torch was shone in his face.

"Where to *sah*?"

The soldier hovered behind the policeman reminding drivers and passengers alike of the lethal force lying beneath the thin veneer of cordiality. Amos could not see the soldier's face but he could feel his hawk eyes watching his every move.

"Visiting relatives, sir."

"*Kuti?*"

"Kitwe, Boss."

"Licence and registration?"

Amos calmly reached into his shirt pocket and produced his identification papers. Grabbing the documents, the policeman shone his torch on them. Then he leant forward and shone his torch into the car, blinding each of the men in turn. Nobody said a word.

With a grunt, the officer gave Amos back his documents and tapped the roof of the car. "You can go." He stepped back. He seemed to have enjoyed his moment of power.

A palpable wave of relief wafted through the car like a cool breeze. If the officers had asked to see inside the trunk, the jig would have been up. They had ridden their luck and Amos knew it. Come daylight, word about the events at Hinckley Farm would be out and every police officer and his dog would be on high alert.

The pain felt like a nail lodged in the back of Farai's head and he squirmed uncomfortably in the confined, stuffy space. His wrists were tied tightly together behind his back and the rough twine dug into his skin while a hard object stabbed at him with every bump in the road. He didn't know how long he had been unconscious but he could tell they were moving at a high speed. He was cramped and hurting, but he was alive. Trying to recall everything that happened, he remembered a white vehicle and a man lying on the road; the blow to the back of his head and a pair of muddy boots. After that, nothing. Who had done this to him and what did they want? His only asset, and it wasn't his, was the car. He felt a moment of panic. What would his boss say? Then relief, maybe the farmer would call the police. But he wasn't expected back for a week. By then it might be too late. He couldn't be kidnapped for money, was it for *umuti?* Would they kill him? His chest bottled with fear and his eyes filled as he thought about his wife and his daughters. What would become of them?

"Hail Mary full of Grace the Lord is with thee…" He began to murmur. All he could do now was to place his life in the hands of God who chose when and where a man would take his last breath.

❋

After they had travelled a few kilometres, Amos suddenly swung the vehicle off the tarred road and onto a dirt track and they slithered into the darkness, tall trees on either side. Low hanging branches and tall reeds slapped against the windows and the body of the vehicle. The four men hardly spoke to one another, the determination of the driver indisputable. They were racing against the daylight.

Amos peered at the dashboard. Dawn in less than an hour. He needed to find a safe place to hide the car, so they could wait the day out before making their next move. He slowed down and turned right into some dense thickets. They could get stuck. The ground was rocky and uneven, but he had to risk it. Amos shifted into low gear and pressed his foot on the accelerator. The car wheezed but he willed it forward. After several minutes of bumping and cajoling the vehicle forward, he stopped and switched off the engine. Amos then instructed the men to go back and cover their tracks as best they could. Then they would all wait in the thick long grass and prickly acacia scrub until the coast was clear.

❋

Inside the boot, Farai had felt the roughness of the ride and every movement hurt. Bruise on bruise. He also sensed that with every lurch in the road, his end was approaching. Hours of pain, discomfort and fear increased his sense of vulnerability. He wanted to weep, certain he would never see his wife and family again. He prayed with growing intensity. "Dear Lord Almighty, if you are there, if you listen to the prayers of your people … Lord, I beg of you, spare me a horrible end. For the sake of my wife, my children, spare me."

Then, suddenly, the vehicle stopped. He heard doors opening. The muffled voices of men followed. Farai's bladder felt full, so full that it was ready to burst.

8

DAY 1
Friday, July 20th 1979

3

Man for the Job

7:32 a.m.

Lusaka City Centre

Detective Maxwell Chanda rolled down the window of his Land Rover. Street hawkers swarmed around him. *"Mpelako Daily Mail,"* he said pointing to a stack of newspapers being sold by a boy who looked older than his frame suggested, and counting out a few coins. Jostling to the front, another urchin thrust a copy of the *Times* in the policeman's face.

"Shiteniko na Times bosses! *Tulyeko naifwe!"* The boy implored but Max shooed him away as he rolled the window up and fixed his gaze on the car in front of him. It bothered him that his exchanges with street vendors were always so curt, but in a country as poor as Zambia, no individual could solve the problems of the destitute and unemployed.

Yet again, the main stories were all about Queen Elizabeth's impending visit to open the Fifth Commonwealth Heads of Government Meeting in Livingstone. The first of its kind on African soil, it was a great source of pride. Everyone, from the president down, seemed giddy with excitement. It would be the Queen's second visit to Zambia. Her first had been to attend the Independence Day celebration in October 1964. Max recalled the grainy black and white photographs. The young, plain-faced monarch stood beside

9

Kenneth Kaunda, the nation's first black president, and before a jubilant crowd as the Union Jack was lowered and the new Zambian flag hoisted up.

Max glanced at the newspaper in his lap and snorted, 'Nation Awaits Queen's Second Visit'. He couldn't understand the fuss. Surely, there were more pressing matters for the country to concern itself with? The monarch's visit would do nothing to improve the lives of the little tykes peddling newspapers on the streets instead of going to school. He watched as the boys darted from one vehicle to the next. Then the light changed, Max shifted gears and followed a rusty old Renault spewing blue fumes.

Max arrived at Lusaka Central Police Station to the rhythmic sound of Jennifer Yumbe's typewriter. The mechanical chattering of her spring-loaded keyboard was punctuated by the occasional swish of a slider. It was a familiar soundtrack inside the shared office space. Jennifer sat upright at her desk with a perfectly symmetrical Afro encircling her pretty face. She had now completed a year at Central Police Headquarters. Max recalled the stir the twenty-three--year-old had generated when she first joined the team. Miss Yumbe, a graduate fresh from Chiswa Secretarial College, had instantly become an object of desire to married and unmarried officers alike, but she rebuffed all advances. Her insistence on professionalism in the male-dominated environment had stoked the ire of some of his colleagues but had earned her the respect of Detective Chanda.

"Morning Sir," Jennifer said, pausing for a moment to look up at her boss. The desks in the office were arranged in the shape of a 'U' with Max's desk at the centre, flanked by Jennifer to one side and Detective Ronald Siatwinda on the other. The latter, Max's loyal deputy, was a smart young man, always eager to please, but not always very thoughtful.

"Morning Miss Yumbe," Max replied as he made his way past a small group of men and women huddled together on wooden benches just inside the door to the office. They lowered their heads avoiding eye contact in deference to him.

Ronald was seated behind his desk speaking to a large woman

wearing a *chitenge* with a matching *doek*. Ronald rudely interrupted the plaintiff in mid-sentence to greet his boss. Max nodded in acknowledgement as he circled his paper-riddled desk to settle in his seat.

"Sir, there's a message from Chief Mbewe," Jennifer told Max as he lowered himself into his chair. "He said to see him as soon as you arrived." The Chief rarely summoned people to his office unless it was something important.

"Did he say what about?"

Ronald again cut off the heavyset woman in mid-sentence. "No, boss. He just said you should see him as soon as you got in." Max busied himself for a moment, straightening a few loose papers and files on his desk before getting up. He wondered what the chief wanted. Not, he felt, a good start to his morning.

❀

"Enter!" Came a deep voice from behind the frosted glass door. Max turned the knob and stepped into the office. The chief was with his secretary, Mrs Zulu, a stern-faced woman who suffered no fools and jealously guarded Chief Mbewe. Before anyone could see him, they had to make an arrangement with her, never a small or pleasant feat.

"Come in Max!" Chief Mbewe raised a hand to wave him inside. "We're just finishing up." Mrs Zulu ostentatiously flicked a page in her ring-bound, shorthand pad and stood up, gathering her possessions and sending Max an 'I'm watching you' glance as she walked towards the door.

Chief Mbewe was an admirer of old-style British aristocrats. He fancied himself a gentleman of the era when men wore cravats, cummerbunds and tail coats. He sported a bushy moustache and impressive sideburns. "Sit, sit." He pointed impatiently to an empty chair. Max obliged.

"Thank you, sir. I heard you wanted to see me?" Max cleared his throat.

Chief Mbewe took a deep breath and shifted uncomfortably. Digging his elbows into the armrests of his chair, he sighed. "Yes.

I'm afraid something dreadful has happened." He leaned forward to pick up a loose sheet of paper. "There's been an incident at Hinckley Farm. It occurred last night." His tone was measured. "I'm sure you know of the Hinckleys, don't you?"

Max nodded. Everyone knew of the Hinckleys. A white couple who owned a commercial farm in the Makeni area, just south of the capital. He recalled that they had come to Zambia well before Independence, and stayed. And who could forget the infamous Women's Brigade incident of 1960 when a young Laura Hinckley had joined a throng of topless African women protesting against white minority rule at the international airport? She had made headlines. 'A British woman bearing her naked breasts in solidarity with a band of indigenous Africans fighting against colonial rule'. It had been quite a story and the British government was not amused. In fact, they were incensed. What had made it worse was that Laura was married to Henry Hinckley, a nephew of then British Home Secretary, one Rab Butler. It was an embarrassment of the highest order!

Chief Mbewe cracked his knuckles. "Yes, I'm afraid a bunch of savages broke into their home last night and bludgeoned them to death in their bedroom. Horrific stuff! Who would do such a thing? … Kill innocent people in their home, while they're sleeping?"

"That's truly shocking, sir…"

Max tried to remember when he had last seen the Hinckleys – it must have been four, even five years ago? It was at a Heroes and Unity Day celebration hosted by President Kaunda in the State House grounds. Max had had to deputise for Chief Mbewe who was ill. The Hinckleys had been the only white couple sitting at the high table with other distinguished guests, all of whom were being honoured for their contributions to the nation, and they had been in high spirits.

Chief Mbewe continued. "A report came in early this morning. Apparently, the housemaid was first to arrive at the scene and she ran to call the foreman after discovering …" he paused, "the mess. … Yes, it's just a horrible, horrible mess." He shook his head several times. "Reporters haven't got to the story yet but I'm sure they'll be all over it by the end of the day." A sliver of disdain for the press crossed his face.

"Do we have any idea yet on who could have done it? Any clues so far, sir?"

The Chief shook his head. "Makeni Police have apprehended a suspect for questioning but … but I can't trust those bumbling idiots. They have botched many cases in the past and this is one we can't afford to mess up!" He clenched his fists. "I need a swift and competent investigation to be performed, and for that I need a detective from the city, not those villagers. One would think some of them never went through the academy." Max kept silent as his boss gathered himself. "Chanda, I need you to personally take on this case, do you hear me? Once the newspapers get a hold of the story everyone will want answers and I don't want us caught flat-footed, like fools. The Hinckleys are – were – very respected, and we need to be seen to be handling this in a professional manner. No hiccups or missteps, eh?" He raised a finger of warning.

"Of course! Yes, sir." An image of the couple lying lifeless on their bed, its sheets caked in blood sent a chill running down Max's spine. He had had his share of gruesome crime scenes. He shut his eyes and shook his head. The things people do to those they love. But this was not a crime of passion.

"I want you to catch all the culprits, and make them sorry, you understand me? You must move quickly, *ukwikusha umutali, kubangilila.*" Chief Mbewe only resorted to his home language in moments of intense emotion. He leant into his chair. "Mrs Hinckley and her husband, are considered national treasures for having stood by us during the freedom struggle. We *must* bring these savages to book for what they've done!"

Max nodded. "Yes, sir, you can count on me." He had hoped for a quiet morning catching up on paperwork. So much for that. "Are there any relatives whom we should inform?"

The Chief shook his head. "Not that I know of, but you'll have to check. As I understand it, all their family is in England. No children either. We'll, of course, need to engage the British High Commission, but leave that one to me." He paused again for a moment, trawling his mind for anything else he might have forgotten and then shook his head. "It's a terrible mess, terrible!"

4

Hinckley Farm

A narrow dirt road ran from the main Lusaka-Kafue trunk road to Hinckley Farm. The dusty thoroughfare was flanked on either side by leafy trees and sprawling scrub. Max and Ronald Siatwinda hardly spoke as they bumped uneasily down the uneven surface for about a kilometre. At last, the dense bush opened up to reveal well-cultivated farmland. They drove beneath a welded archway engraved with the words 'HINCKLEY FARM', passing various outbuildings, and catching a whiff of animal manure. Max had worked on his uncle's small farm as a boy and was all too familiar with the smell, and the restless sound of livestock in their pens. A thin, uniformed police officer, who had been sitting outside the farmhouse on a wooden stool, stood up at the sight of their approaching vehicle. A group of farmworkers, a few men and some women and children were sitting quietly on a grassy patch on the other side of the driveway. Max parked his car in front of the farmhouse noticing as he did so that the workers' quarters, small breeze-block homes, stood about a mile from the main homestead.

"Morning *bwana*!" The uniformed officer saluted.

Max nodded, "I am Detective Maxwell Chanda from Lusaka Central Police. And you are?"

"Pethias, *sah* … Officer Pethias Haachambwa." The young man pulled himself up and saluted again.

"Are you the only one here, manning the house?"

"No, *sah*." Max raised his eyebrows, and the young man continued, "My partner has just gone … for few minutes only, *sah*. He come back now, now, now, *sah.*"

Max felt a recurrent sense of dismay. This was their police force. Here at a murder scene. A couple of awkward young men, with little training, few skills and no obvious motivation. This was how it was now. Young people took what they could find, choices were few, more especially for the poor and unskilled.

Max scanned the area across the gravel driveway – the gathering of farmworkers were sitting quietly, curious and afraid in equal measure. Looking down at his feet, Max noticed numerous footprints on the dusty ground. Had the workers crowded around the scene or had it simply been the police, over-active in their haste to search the surrounding area for clues?

"Where are the bodies?" Ronald asked impatiently – eager, as always, to impress his superior. Pethias adjusted his oversized hat and pointed towards the farmhouse to his left. "Inside, *sah* ... but we *oloso* find *somuthingie kunyumba bwana.*" He said pointing to the back of the house.

Max raised his head. "Show me."

They followed the young officer along a concrete drain that ran the length of the house. The walls of the house had numerous termite tracks snaking over the surface. Reaching the back of the building, Max noticed a trail of blood on the ground leading up to an area enclosed by a wire fence. Just outside the enclosed area lay the bodies of two dogs. The boerboels had clearly been hacked to death by something sharp, perhaps a machete, but who would do such a thing?

He once again noted the presence of footprints in the dry, dusty soil similar to those he had seen at the front of the house.

"Have any weapons been found?" Max looked at Pethias, "Did you look, or did anyone tell you to look?" The young man shook his head. It was not clear if they hadn't found anything, or hadn't looked. The two detectives spent several minutes scanning the area for anything else that might be of use. Finally, Max turned again to Pethias and said. "A thorough search of the entire grounds will need to be conducted, but first I want to start with the inside of the house.

Take us to where they entered."

The young officer led the way back to the front of the house. As they reached the spot where they began, Max looked at the footprints in the soil again. "Since you arrived, has anyone other than the police gone into the house?" He asked. Pethias lowered his head sheepishly.

Ronald pressed him. "*Alah iwe*, answer the question!"

"Yah *sah* ... only foreman *sah* ... to cover up bodies, *bwana*." Pethias rubbed the back of his neck.

Ronald was impatient with him. "*Buti iwe*, don't you understand that by letting people into the house you may have compromised the crime scene or even destroyed crucial evidence?"

Max raised his hand gently. He made a mental note to talk to Ronald afterwards about his impetuous nature, no good would come out of badgering the poor young man – he had probably never received adequate training on how to properly secure a crime scene.

"Can you take us to the bodies?" Max asked calmly.

"Yes, *sah*!" Pethias turned quickly and led the way to the front of the house, his baggy khaki shorts hovering above his knees.

The three men were soon standing outside the entrance to the farmhouse where there were clear signs of forced entry. The front door and the frame were splintered, perhaps by a crowbar or a wrench, and now dangled off one hinge.

"Did you touch anything?" Ronald asked the young officer, who scratched his temple nervously and mumbled. The detective raised his eyebrows, as if nothing more could be expected from the rural police.

The entrance opened directly into a living room with parquet flooring. A discoloured rug lay between two sofas. The floor was littered with broken pieces of porcelain. Several side tables lay on their sides. A wooden entertainment centre had been pulled away from a wall and a television set lay cracked on the floor. Had the assailants been searching for something? Max stopped in front of a framed wedding photograph of a young white couple – a frozen vignette of a happier time.

"Looks like they ransacked the place," Ronald said, stating the obvious. A quick foray into the adjoining dining room revealed signs of a similar violent disorder. Henry Hinckley was frail, and disabled by a stroke, Laura was small, and certainly not young. What on earth had gone on, Max wondered. What might have caused such disarray in the living room as well as the dining room?

A door just off the latter led into a small kitchen. Max and Ronald scanned the room, everything looked neat and orderly, it would seem the assailants had not disturbed the kitchen.

"Are the bodies in the master bedroom?" Max asked, as the three men stood at the mouth of the corridor leading to the bedrooms. There were doors on either side of the narrow corridor and a door at the far end of it. Officer Pethias nodded. "Yes, *sah*, dey are in bedroom, *sah*." He pointed to the door at the end of the corridor before adjusting his hat once again and leading the way.

The door to the Hinckley's main bedroom was made from thin sheets of plywood. It showed no signs of damage, but it was obvious how easily it could have been pushed open. Max lingered at the door, trying to imagine how terrified the couple would have been. But if they had locked the door and were sheltering inside, why the violence in the two other rooms? It made no sense.

Pethias pushed the door slowly and stepped inside the room, Max followed behind him and then took a few more steps past the young officer. He was immediately struck with a sense of horror. There was blood everywhere. On the sheets, on the floor, on the walls … And then Max heard a retching sound behind him and turned quickly. Ronald was bent over with one hand against the wall. Pethias moved to his aid. "*Yah-yah, bwana, muli bwino?*"

"Go, outside," Max said more peremptorily than he intended. "Take a break, get some air, and when you're ready, come back and join me."

Max turned to the room again, it was in a mess. There was a thin bloodied bedsheet covering a body on a queen-sized bed to his left. To Max's right, near the foot of a dressing table and a few feet from the open doors of a wardrobe, lay the body of Laura Hinckley. Her head and torso were covered by a *chitenge*. At the foot of the

18

wardrobe was a pile of clothes and a small rectangular wooden panel as well as a metal safe lying ajar and empty. Max examined the area closely. Who could have done this? What happened, what were they looking for? Stepping closer and careful not to touch anything, he reached Laura's body.

"Apart from covering the bodies, did you or anyone move anything in this room?"

Pethias shook his head. "No, *sah*." His response was timid.

"Are you sure?" Max turned his head towards the young man. Pethias silently lowered his head.

Max knew the results of the formal autopsy would take weeks. This was his only chance to try and interpret precisely what had happened. He squatted down, pinched the edge of the *chitenge* and pulled the cloth back slowly, then quickly covered his mouth. Officer Pethias gave an audible gasp and averted his eyes. Whoever had committed this atrocity, had been brutal.

Max took a deep breath pulled out a small ring-bound notepad that he always carried in his top pocket and began a slow, meticulous examination of the bodies, his eyes going over every detail.

There were deep gashes in the head, neck, limbs and abdomen of both victims. The couple were mutilated almost beyond recognition. He could not remember a more savage attack. Noting every detail, he paused every few seconds to scribble into his notepad: deep cuts to the left clavicle, cranium, throat and both forearms of the female victim, possibly made by a machete, perhaps the same weapon used to bludgeon the two dogs outside. Evidence of severe bruising to the face, indicating a possible struggle with her assailant or assailants. Max was relieved to see that there were no signs of sexual assault. Laura's dressing gown, wrapped loosely around her, was soaked in blood. It seemed likely that she had bled to death. Henry lay on the bed, his left arm dangling over the edge and with multiple lacerations on his abdomen, as well as a deep gash on the right of his cranium and another on his chest. Max examined the hands of each victim – the woman had traces of what might have been skin beneath the fingernails of her right hand – had she scratched her assailant?

Would any such scratches still be visible? So he continued, noting each detail, each question as it occurred to him.

Finally, Max stood up and stretched. He looked down at the pile of clothes on the floor and the empty safe next to a rectangular wooden panel. He took the few steps to the wardrobe and craned his neck inside it. There was a rectangular recess at the bottom, which he figured had been covered by the wooden panel that now lay on the floor. What had been hidden in that safe?

Max spent the next hour combing the room for clues and taking notes in an attempt to piece together the series of events that had led to so much violence and death.

While Max was in the house, Ronald, embarrassed by his momentary weakness, had taken the initiative to summon the housemaid who had discovered the break-in earlier that morning. Her name was Nawakwi and she lived in the farmworkers' compound. One of the farm-hands had gone to fetch her, and she arrived shortly before Max emerged, his face drawn, Pethias in his wake. He nodded at Ronald, and made his way to a patch of shade, where he drew out a cigarette, and allowed himself a few minutes to compose himself. He felt very shaken. The personal aggression manifested here was on a scale that he had never seen before, and he couldn't think why. What had happened to make a burglary go so wrong? What were they searching for? Why had there been a need to kill the victims? They could simply have been tied up. It was clear several men had been involved. Presumably young fit men? Had they a grudge against the Hinckleys? They were not known as unfair employers.

Taking one last pull of his cigarette, he dropped it on the ground and crushed it in the dirt. Then he walked over to where Ronald stood underneath a guava tree with the housemaid who was obviously frightened. Across the driveway, several children were playing a game of hop-scotch. Max watched as the two little girls skipped and jumped, blissfully unaware of the tragedy in their midst.

The maid, a slender young woman wore a plain grey dress and a *doek*. Her face was drawn as if exhausted from shedding tears.

"This is Nawakwi?" Ronald told Max. A gust of July wind lifted the hem of her dress slightly, the girl quickly caught it and pressed her skirt down before genuflecting to show respect to the two authority figures standing in front of her.

"Your full name?" Ronald asked.

She kept her eyes fixed to a point near his feet. "Nawakwi Evelyn N'gambi."

Max examined her closely. He placed great stock on first impressions and his first impression was that Nawakwi looked unremarkable and honest. "You work – worked – for Mr and Mrs Hinckley?" Max began. She nodded. "Can you tell us exactly what you saw this morning? I want you to describe every detail in the same way that you did when you spoke with the officers at Makeni this morning."

Ronald pulled out a small notepad. Nawakwi kept her eyes trained to the ground and said nothing. Seeing her hesitation, Max rephrased the question in Bemba. Nawakwi lifted her head slowly, clearly more comfortable with her home language, and began to describe what she had seen.

She had arrived at the farmhouse shortly before 5 a.m. as usual. She had used her key to enter through the back door to the kitchen. Max asked if she had seen anything untoward in the backyard, had she not seen the two dogs? Nawakwi said that it was still dark at the time and she had not seen anything. Besides, it was not unusual for Chanter and Whisky to have wandered off somewhere on the farm near the pig sty or the hatchery. She went on to tell them how she had filled the kettle with water and set it on the stove to make the morning tea. Mrs Hinckley liked to wake up to her tea. She had gone on to clean a few cups and plates left overnight in the sink before opening the door and walking into the adjoining dining room to find it in complete disarray. She was frightened. Her first impulse was to go and call the foreman for help. Max could tell that she was shaken.

Ronald asked why she had not gone to check on Mr and Mrs Hinckley. Max was growing impatient with his young detective, it was obvious that the girl would have been too frightened to do such a thing. Max turned to Officer Pethias, "Go and see if you can find the foreman …"

"*Bashi* Joshua." Nawakwi completed Max's sentence.

"I'd like to talk to him." Max said.

Pethias quickly put a hand to his head in salute. "*Shuwa, shuwa bwana* … right away." He hurried off in the direction of the farmworkers gathered across the dusty driveway.

Max turned back to the young housemaid and continued his line of questions in Bemba. Nawakwi described how she had found *bashi* Joshua, the foreman, with several farmworkers preparing feed for the chickens in the hatchery and they immediately all ran back to the house. When they arrived at the front, they noticed immediately that the door was splintered and hanging loosely off one of the hinges. Nawakwi had been too afraid to go inside, it was *bashi* Joshua who had entered the dwelling and eventually discovered the bodies. Her eyes filled with tears as she recounted the moment the foreman had told her what he had found inside. Madame and *bwana* Hinckley had always been good to her.

The foreman had a tall muscular frame and the thick broad hands of one who earned his living through manual labour. He too appeared shaken by what he had witnessed.

"Describe exactly what you saw, it's important that you tell me everything." Max said. *Bashi* Joshua, whose full name was Otis Lifuti, went on to tell the detectives how he had walked into the living room to find it in a shambles. Furniture tossed all over the place, the television smashed, side tables turned. He had called out to the Hinckleys by name, but there had been no answer. Fearing the worst, he had walked further into the house. Like the living room, the dining room was also in a mess. He proceeded down the hallway and reaching the main bedroom, he had stood outside the door and called them again.

"Was the door closed?" Max asked.

Bashi Joshua thought about it for a moment before shaking his head. "No, it was open, but not completely. I remember pushing it open."

Ronald chimed in. "And then what did you do?"

Bashi Joshua hesitated. "… I went inside and found them." Max recalled the state of the bodies lying in the bedroom, it was a lot for anyone to take, even a strongman like the foreman.

Max looked straight at *bashi* Joshua, "Was either of them still alive?"

He shook his head. "No, sir. Not as far as I could tell."

The two detectives then went on to ask for details about where in the room he had found the bodies and how they were positioned. The foreman said that Mr Hinckley had been lying flat on his back on the right side of the bed with his left arm dangling over the edge. Mrs Hinckley was on the floor at the feet of the dressing table with her right forearm covering part of her face as if making one final attempt at shielding herself from a fatal blow. They asked whether or not he had seen the safe, the clothes on the floor and the rectangular wooden panel. His observations were consistent with what they had found. Ronald scribbled everything down in his notepad. Max also asked the foreman about the bedsheet covering Mr Hinckley as well as the *chitenge* over Mrs Hinckley's body. *Bashi* Joshua confessed that it was he who had covered the bodies of his employers out of a sense of respect for the dead – he could not bear to leave *bwana* and madam Hinckley like that. Seeing the anguish on his face, both Max and Ronald resisted the urge to admonish him for his final act of compassion towards his employers.

Max looked into the distance at the breeze-block farmworker homes. They were a fair distance away, but surely someone must have seen a vehicle approaching the house in the middle of the night? The foreman shook his head. Neither he nor any of the other workers had seen or heard anything. Max cast his eyes ahead at the winding driveway which led from the main road to the farmhouse. There could only be one explanation, the assailants had driven part of the way, perhaps with their headlamps turned off, and then walked the rest of the way undetected.

When they had exhausted their questions, they instructed *bashi* Joshua and Nawakwi to remain on the farm. They were not to leave until a full police investigation had taken place. Max and Ronald then began walking towards their vehicle, each absorbed in his own thoughts, Officer Pethias trailing in their wake. They were halfway up the driveway when another young officer appeared, quickening his steps into a trot as he drew towards them.

"That is my partner, *sah*!" Pethias announced, relief in his voice. "Officer Fackson Malunga."

"I've come from Makeni Police Station," Malunga panted, slightly out of breath. "They have a suspect… it's the driver *sah*!"

5

The Driver

Makeni Police Outpost

Makeni Police Station was no more than a remote satellite outpost. A solitary room served as both an office and sleeping quarters for whichever junior officer was on duty. A desk with some tattered folders stood in one corner, a thin narrow mattress in the other. About thirty metres behind the office was a small holding cell where the supposedly guilty were stashed like unclean clothes. It abutted a pit latrine whose foul smell offered an additional punishment to the incarcerated.

"We'll bring him out now-now, *sah!*" an over-eager corporal shouted. Max and Ronald stood outside the door to the station. It had been a long day, and Max was anxious to get back to HQ to find out if there had been any other developments. How easy it would be if Elijah Nkole, the Hinckley's long-standing driver, were the culprit. Max was determined to keep an open mind, but to him it seemed unlikely. Nawakwi, had told them that he was the man trusted with ferrying their money and depositing it into their bank account every month. Why would a man who had served the Hinckleys loyally for many years suddenly turn around and commit such a heinous crime? It didn't add up.

In Max's estimation, the officers at Makeni had never had to deal with a murder before, let alone a murder of a well-known white couple who knew the president. Enthusiastic, ill-trained and eager to please, they had quickly concluded that the driver Elijah Nkole was responsible.

Within minutes, a shirtless, haggard, barefooted man was dragged in front of Max and Ronald. The two detectives glanced at each other. The man had already been taken through his paces. He had a gash above his left eye and a swollen lower lip. His hands were tied behind his back as the over-eager corporal prodded him in the back.

"*Apa, apa!* Sit, sit, *apa*! *Ikala, apa, kammani!*" The corporal yelled, pointing to a dusty spot next to the police station building. Elijah glanced painfully at the two detectives before sitting down on the hard floor, his feet splayed in front of him, his body angled uncomfortably to accommodate his hands pinned behind his back.

Max turned to the corporal. "Undo the handcuffs," he ordered.

After a brief silence, Ronald was the first to ask a question. "Is your name Elijah … Elijah Nkole, driver to Mr and Mrs Hinckley?" Elijah breathed heavily, his eyes were trained to a spot on the ground between his legs. "Are you Elijah Nkole?" Ronald repeated raising his voice.

The young corporal was impatient. "*Basopo iwe*! *Kamba manje!* Otherwise *Nizakumenya mbama!*" He threatened before lifting his foot to nudge Elijah on the shoulder with the soles of his leather boots.

Max had had enough of the corporal's brazen show of cruelty. "Step back! There's no need for that!" The corporal took a step back, his face was pregnant with a protest that he dared not voice. "Go and bring me the written statements that you gathered from all the people you interviewed this morning." Clearly unhappy, the corporal retreated to the small office to gather the papers.

Elijah raised his head slowly, perhaps grateful for Max's merciful gesture. His eyes were ruby red.

"You are Elijah Nkole, the driver to Mr and Mrs Hinckley?" Max asked.

Elijah finally nodded. "Yes sir … I am, but … but I had nothing to do with …" His words seemed to die in his throat and he lowered his head again. Max noticed Elijah's good command of the English language. This was to be expected from a person who had been one of the Hinckley's most trusted hands.

Ronald inched forward. "Where were you last night, between the hours of midnight and three o'clock in the morning?"

"I – I was at home, sir … sleeping. My wife and children can tell you. I – I swear to you, as God is my witness, I had nothing to do with any of this."

"What of the safe in the bedroom?" Ronald continued. "You're the only person who they trusted with their money to deposit it in their account every month. What happened to the money?" They waited while Elijah shook his head slowly from side to side.

"I've worked for Mr and Mrs Hinckley for seven years. Mr Hinckley taught me how to drive, Mrs Hinckley even paid for my licence … why would I … why would I turn around and …" Tears welled in his eyes. If this was an act, he was doing a masterful job. Yet, Max sighed inwardly, the man was tired, hungry, frightened and he'd clearly been beaten badly. Under such circumstances, tears might come easily. Still, it did not seem conceivable that Elijah would suddenly brutally murder his employers for money that if he'd wanted he could have acquired more easily. The ignorant and over-zealous rural officers had most certainly jumped to conclusions.

The corporal soon returned holding some loose sheets of papers in his hand. "Is this all of them?" Max asked. The officer nodded as he gave them to Ronald. Max paused for a moment, deep in thought. He knew that he would have to work on gathering new written statements because nothing that the village policemen had obtained could be trusted. "I want you to gather his shoes and any possessions he has here and bring him to the car. I don't want any nasty business." Max raised his eyebrows, "Understand! I'm transferring him to Central, we'll take it from there." The two detectives walked slowly back to their vehicle and sat in silence for a moment.

"What next boss? Back to Central?" Ronald asked breaking the silence.

Max nodded before placing his key into the ignition. "I think so. We've seen all we can here for now. Let's go back to the station and regroup. We'll need to send a vehicle in the morning to pick up the housemaid and the foreman from the farm. We'll need to properly document their statements. We can't afford to make any mistakes." He looked up and saw Elijah being led towards the car by the corporal. Max turned the key and the Land Rover roared into life. Leaning forward, Max adjusted the dial to his AM radio. The crackle of static filled the air as he searched for a signal. He settled on Radio 1 where he heard the distinct voice of the nation's president, Kenneth Kaunda, being interviewed by a foreign news correspondent.

"… *your Excellency sir, what are your thoughts on her Majesty Queen Elizabeth's impending visit to Zambia? I believe this will be her first visit since Zambia gained its independence in 1964?*"

President Kaunda sounded as regal as always. "*Indeed, we are delighted to welcome her back to Zambia. Our two nations share a much storied past and it's important that we maintain a cordial and healthy relationship. Yes, indeed all Zambians, including myself, are excited about her upcoming visit.*"

Max sucked his teeth. It seemed to him like he could not escape talk of Queen Elizabeth's visit, no matter how hard he tried – it was all the news in the country.

6

It Flows Downhill

Central Police Station, Lusaka

Max and Ronald arrived back at Lusaka Central Police Station shortly after three o'clock in the afternoon. On the journey back from Makeni, they had discussed what they'd seen and what to do next. It was Ronald's opinion that the crime was most likely orchestrated, or at least facilitated, by someone who knew the Hinckleys well. One of the workers perhaps, a farmhand, Elijah the driver or even the young housemaid Nawakwi. In his estimation whoever had committed the crime had been searching for something in particular, something inside the safe, perhaps? If that was the case, then surely one or more of the Hinckley's workers had a hand in it. Ronald suspected that Elijah was their man – a few more days of tough interrogation and he believed that Elijah would confess and reveal the names of his accomplices. However, Max was not convinced of this theory. The Hinckleys were good employers and in his experience of working on his uncle's farm, he recalled that farmworkers were generally timorous in nature. It was hard to imagine that they would be involved in such a brutal killing. Yes, Elijah had access to the house, and he might be said to have a motive – the money – but surely it was a flawed plan to stage a robbery knowing that fingers would ultimately point at you? Besides, if it was money he was after, why wouldn't he have made plans to ship his family away weeks before and then run off with the money in the morning on his way to the bank?

He shook his head. Surely, the assumption that 'money was the root of all evil' was reductionist, even if they did live in a country where most people were poor. Most people were poor, yes, but like most poor people, honest.

Max did have suspicions about the housemaid. Not directly, he was sure. But she might have known there was a safe or at least something valuable in the room and inadvertently told somebody about it. One thing the two detectives agreed on was that the murders were surely the result of a robbery gone awry. Perhaps Mrs Hinckley had resisted handing over their valuables? Or even attempted to fight back? Certainly, more workers needed to be questioned and they would need to send out a notice to all the police outposts in the district to see if anyone had noticed anything untoward in the past few days or weeks. From all his years as a detective, Max knew that someone always knew something or saw something. It was practically impossible for a crime to be committed without anyone seeing or hearing anything. There was no such thing as a perfect crime and this one – with all its signs of violence, and crude haste – was certainly not one such.

The two policemen met Jennifer Yumbe at the top of the stairs. She seemed surprised to see them.

"Oh, Detective Chanda, good afternoon sir … I wasn't expecting you so soon." She adjusted the strap of her handbag over her shoulder. "I'm just on my way to a late lunch break." Ignoring Ronald altogether, she fixed her gaze on the older man. Max had long sensed the young woman's contempt for his junior officer; he could tell that she did not much care for him but he had not yet determined why.

Jennifer cleared her throat. "Sir, Chief Mbewe sent for you again around noon. He said that you should proceed to his office immediately on your return."

Max screwed up his face. "He wants to see me again? But we spoke this morning."

"Yes, sir. He said he wanted to see you again – as soon as you returned."

"Thank you, Miss Yumbe." Max nodded, he never referred to her by her first name, determining always to maintain a professional distance between himself and the staff who worked under him.

"I'm just running to buy some lunch. I'll return to my desk in a moment, sir." Max nodded again and the young woman hurried down the steps.

Chief Mbewe had a visitor with him, a tall white gentleman in an expensive grey suit who exuded a quiet confidence that for some reason irked the older detective. The Chief made introductions. "Detective Maxwell Chanda, meet the Honourable Peter James from the British High Commissioner's office.

"Peter, please call me Peter."

"Ah, yes, Peter… This is Maxwell Chanda, one of our most experienced detectives."

The three men took their seats, and the Chief continued, "Max, Peter has brought a rather sensitive matter to my attention." He ran his fingers over his chin. "Concerning Mr and Mrs Hinckley." Max straightened his back. Peter crossed and uncrossed his legs. "As I think you're aware, Henry Hinckley is … was a nephew to former British Home Secretary, the Honourable Rab Butler."

Max remained silent, it was the first he'd heard of this relationship and he didn't know what the significance might be to the case in hand. "Yes, well…" Chief Mbewe continued, "this presents a rather complicated situation – what with Queen Elizabeth's forthcoming visit in a week's time."

Peter James shifted in his seat, and raised his right hand, "Yes, London received news of the tragedy at Hinckley Farm in the early hours of the morning. There's concern, much concern that the investigation be handled professionally." Max twitched with irritation. He knew it was the protocol for a diplomatic mission to get involved whenever one of its nationals was killed under dubious circumstances but the condescension in this man's tone rankled him. When would the British learn that a Zambian professional was every bit as competent as a British officer, or at least, he hoped so?

Peter cleared his throat. "Given the very sensitive situation in Rhodesia, and Zambia's support of the liberation movements, The Home Office is concerned that there should be no negative press reports in the run-up to the Commonwealth Heads of Government Summit in a week's time." Chief Mbewe nodded sagely as if he too were fully apprised of the delicacy of diplomatic issues. Peter then turned and looked at Max, "The murder of the Hinckleys has the potential to stir anxieties about Her Majesty's safety. There are already safety concerns as I've indicated. Now the press will report that Rab Butler's nephew has been murdered..." He shook his head, and turned to look at Chief Mbewe. "I have come here charged with the explicit instruction to ensure that all the culprits are apprehended and brought to justice immediately. This issue cannot loom over Her Majesty's trip, we simply can't have it overshadowing the royal visit. The British public will simply not tolerate it!"

Max nodded and looked at his boss. Chief Mbewe gestured for him to continue. "Mr James," he looked at Mbewe, "Sir, we are already on the case, it may take some time but we will get to the bottom of it. We will round up the culprits, of that I am sure."

"Yes, but how long will it take?" Peter asked sharply. Max bit back his irritation. Clearly the British representative was as used to being obeyed as he had no appreciation of the complexities of a murder enquiry. Did he expect them just to round up a few men to satisfy the demands of the British government?

Max hesitated, trying his best to suppress annoyance. "A few weeks... it depends on how quickly we can get suspects to talk and where they might be. We have a person of interest in custody already but we have to do a lot more digging. Who knows where they may have..." Peter interrupted him.

"I'm afraid that just won't do, detective. Her Majesty is scheduled to arrive in seven days' time. We'll give you five days, no more. The perpetrators have to be rounded up before she gets on that plane. Failure to do so and we're likely to find ourselves in a diplomatic morass. The London office might just recommend cancelling the whole visit and I'm sure Kaunda would be mightily displeased with that outcome. I'm sure he'd take it as a personal snub." He paused. "Gentlemen, I'm sure I don't need to tell you that our very jobs lie in the balance here, we have to clean this up and clean it up now!"

When Peter James left the office, Chief Mbewe shut the door behind him and sat back into his chair. There was a visible tightness around his mouth, a window into the tension and irritation that he was trying to supress. "Chanda" He said sternly. "I need you to solve this thing, any resources you need, please don't hesitate. You must round up all of these murderers immediately, without delay! I will not be the one to embarrass the Inspector General or indeed His Excellency the President for that matter, you understand? There's a lot riding on this, we cannot have the first ever Commonwealth Heads of Government Summit on African soil disrupted because we can't apprehend some two-bit thugs! If we fail on this one, heads will surely roll and believe me, they say shit only flows one way – and that's downhill!"

Max nodded. He thought it best to keep his mouth shut. He was aware of being very angry. The words of Peter James echoed in his mind: "I have come here charged with the explicit instruction to ensure that all the culprits are apprehended and brought to justice immediately." An order followed by a threat, "Failure to do so and we're likely to find ourselves in a diplomatic morass."

So, this was British justice. "So much for our independence," he thought.

DAY 2
Saturday, July 21st 1979

7

So Many Questions to Answer

1:39 a.m.

Chilenge, Lusaka

There was a light in the distance above him. A set of blurred oblong faces momentarily appeared. He felt the weight of his own body pulling him deeper into an abyss. He tried yelling but found he had no voice. He tried to move, but his muscles were powerless and he could not heave himself upwards. He cried out at the top of his lungs but no sound came and as the faces faded, he sank into a desolate black hole.

Max opened his eyes and sprang into sitting position, his chest heaving. His body was drenched in sweat. He blinked several times as his eyes became accustomed to the space around him. Disoriented, it took a few seconds to find his bearings. Max glanced at his wife, Mavis, who was fast asleep, her back turned towards him. He wiped his brow with the palm of his hand. The night was still, the air dense, which was unusual for July, the windy season. Max took a few deep breaths and stood up reaching for a packet of Rothman's on the night stand. Then, careful not to wake Mavis, he walked quietly out of the room.

In the living room, he found the key to the front door which was hidden in its usual place underneath the record player, a wedding gift from his late uncle, Joshua, who had looked after him after his father's death when Max was just ten years old. Unlocking the front door, Max stepped onto the edge of a concrete verandah. Lighting his cigarette, he drew on it, feeling the bitter taste of tobacco on his tongue. His nightmares had resurfaced following the death of his infant daughter, Lindiwe. She had died in her sleep, almost four months previously. The doctors had been unable to explain it, they said babies just sometimes died in this way. They called it a 'cot death'. But how could a child just die for no reason?

Lindiwe had been their second child, their God-given daughter who had suddenly stopped breathing. Although Mavis had not put it into words, Max knew that she blamed him for what had transpired. It had happened one Saturday afternoon, the first time his wife had decided to leave Lindiwe in his care to attend a local Catholic Women's League meeting. Such fellowship was something that Mavis had always cherished. After four months of staying at home tending her newborn baby, she had asked Max to mind the children for a few hours. She had fed Lindiwe and put her to sleep in her cot before she left, telling Max to listen out for her cry, and to check her regularly, as she did not sleep for very long in the afternoons. Max had checked the tiny girl before settling himself on the verandah for a beer and a smoke. One beer had become two or three, and before he knew it, Mavis was home. And the first thing she asked was about Lindiwe. "When I checked on her, she was sleeping," Max replied, feeling guilty that he had only checked once, before he went to sit outside. They were words he would never forget. Barely a minute later, a shrill cry pierced the tranquil afternoon air.

"*Lindi! We mwana wandi! … Lindi! Lindiwe! Shibuka! We mwana wandi! Shibuka! Shibuka!*"

Max ran into the house to find his wife wailing in anguish, as she held their lifeless baby in her arms. The proverbial bow had broken. Max's nightmares returned to haunt him.

His thoughts travelled back to Hinckley Farm and the sight of the mutilated bodies, the blood-stained bedsheets and the splatter on the walls. What savagery? What insanity?

Before Max had left his office, he had left instructions for a team of officers to travel to the farm first thing in the morning to pick up the foreman and the housemaid and bring them to HQ so that Max could personally record their written statements. He also instructed the officers to gather all the files and documents from the Hinckley's study. He wanted to learn more about the couple – their friends and acquaintances, who they did business with and who had visited them in the last several days and weeks. Max had also arranged for the best fingerprint expert to comb through the entire farmhouse for prints – no one was to enter the building until every room had been dusted for fingerprints. There was also the issue of the getaway car. Max reasoned that the attackers must have used a vehicle of some sort to get to the farm and then to drive as far away from the crime scene as possible, it was the logical thing to do. He had already put out an announcement on national radio and in all the district police stations across the country to be on high alert for any suspicious activity or any stolen or abandoned vehicles. He figured that they had probably ditched the car by now or switched number plates. Max was confident, however, that someone somewhere would have seen or heard something that would prove useful. Also, on his list of priorities for the next day was to ask Nawakwi some more questions. Although he had found her to be credible, he wanted to explore his theory that she may have unwittingly told somebody about the safe in the Hinckley's bedroom and perhaps that had been the motive behind the attack? He also wanted more of the farmworkers questioned; the incident did not have the feel of a random attack and someone must have known something.

Max pulled on his cigarette and slowly released the smoke. He knew he had to go back to bed for he had a long day ahead of him and he had a feeling things would get worse before they got better.

✳

6:42 a.m.

Standing in front of the bathroom mirror, Max ran a wire comb through his thick mat of hair. He could hear Mavis in the kitchen as she prepared his morning meal. He sighed. They had become like strangers in a boarding house – polite to each other while hiding their emotions. He wished he could talk to his wife about Lindiwe, explain how he blamed himself. He had tried to talk to her, but the words always seemed to disappear on the journey from his heart to his lips. He patted his head softly moulding his hair into shape. In the past couple of years streaks of grey had begun to appear behind his temples. He looked at himself in the mirror and straightened his collar before making his way to the kitchen to eat his breakfast.

Mavis carefully placed a metal plate with two slices of buttered bread and a fried egg in front of her husband. Then, she made her way to the back of the house and returned with a pot of boiling water for his tea. Max watched her pour it into his cup, but she did not look up to meet his gaze. That done, Mavis silently left the room into the corridor towards their son's bedroom to get him ready for school. Since their daughter's death, she scarcely engaged in conversations with her husband, choosing instead to immerse herself in caring for their son and in performing her household chores.

The telephone in the living room rang at exactly seven thirty-five, Max glanced at his watch before leaving his seat to answer it.

"Hallo?" He said holding the receiver to his ear.

"Hallo boss, it's me ... Ronald." Max was half expecting Ronald's call – his eagerness to prove himself was predictable and sometimes very useful. "Boss, I just received information about an abandoned vehicle. A white Peugeot station wagon. It was found early this morning about five kilometres east of Hinckley Farm... I think it could be something." There was a hint of triumph in his voice.

Max breathed in, his mind already running laps about what to do next. He would need to get out there with a crew of experts to examine the vehicle, comb it for fingerprints and clues. If it was indeed the vehicle used by the criminals, his suspicions had been correct – the culprits had either abandoned it or switched cars or made their way on foot. Clearing his throat, he said, "Okay, I'll be at the station in twenty minutes," and placed the receiver back onto its cradle. He would wait to see if the find amounted to anything.

❊

9:01 a.m.

Seven kilometres east of Hinckley Farm

The white Peugeot was hidden in a heavily wooded area several yards from a well-trodden footpath. Max, Ronald and a band of uniformed officers trundled through dense brush, trampling over long grass to reach it. Clearly, great care had been taken to place the vehicle out of sight from the dirt track. If it had not been for a small group of village children on their way to set bird traps, it might not have been found for weeks.

Three uniformed officers began to clear the bulk of the foliage as Max and Ronald watched. Then, the former ordered his men to stand back while he drew closer to closely examine the vehicle. Twigs crackled under foot as he inched closer. First, he leaned forward and removed the two last branches that had been lain over the bonnet. There it was, a white Peugeot with a rusted body. He cleared more of the brush away with his hands and looked at the number plate. He pulled out the notepad from his shirt pocket and scribbled it down. He would have it checked out at the station but he could bet the vehicle would come up as stolen. Max stood up and slowly trampled over the surrounding brush until he was standing to the side of the car. Then, careful not to touch anything, he peered through the window. Down, underneath the passenger seat were a set of crowbars and traces of red earth similar to what he recalled seeing around the Hinckley's farmhouse. He turned and panned the scene before him. It was clear to him what had to be done. "*Iwe, iwe na iwe!*" He said pointing to each of the uniformed officers in turn. "Pay attention." He then began to issue instructions. The men should survey each and every inch of the surrounding area for clues, anything the assailants could have dropped or left behind. If there was a shred of evidence, he wanted it!

It took the better part of four hours to comb through the surrounding area looking for anything that might be construed as a clue. Fingerprints were taken from the vehicle. The initial search of the car yielded a set of vehicle registration documents in the glove compartment as well as a smudged petrol receipt book. The set of crowbars were carefully dusted for prints before being wrapped in a plastic bag to take back to Central. There were no visible traces of blood and no signs of a sharp weapon, a knife or a machete that might have been used in the murders. Max mused that the criminals had probably fled with the murder weapon or weapons, but they would surely have wanted to get rid of them as soon as possible. Max knew that the process of getting a match on the fingerprints was an arduous manual process that would likely take several weeks or longer – time they did not have. Besides, fingerprints were only useful if someone was already in the police record books for prior offences. The number plate search would be quicker, all vehicles in the country were registered with the Road Transport and Safety Agency under the Ministry of Transport and Communications.

Later that afternoon when the detectives arrived back at the station, Max immediately sent for the vehicle number plate to be checked against the records at the Ministry. As Max and Ronald stepped back into their office, they found two cardboard boxes of folders on Max's desk.

"Those are the papers you requested yesterday from Hinckley Farm, sir," Jennifer Yumbe said even before Max could ask the question. "They brought them in early this morning."

Max circled his desk. "Very good." He stared at the two piles, arms akimbo. "The best thing to do is to split them between the two of us, you take one and I'll take the other." He looked at Ronald.

"Yes boss, I'll start on it immediately. Is there anything in particular you're looking for?"

Max shook his head. "No, nothing in particular but just go through the papers carefully and see if there's anything that looks strange or doesn't smell right. We may not find anything but you never know, we just have to be thorough, and cover every angle."

"Yes boss, I understand." Ronald picked up one of the boxes and placed it on his desk. He pulled out a manila folder and sat down to leaf through it.

Jennifer cleared her throat. "Sir ... there was also a message from Sergeant Mabushi. The people you summoned for further questioning have arrived."

Max nodded. "Good. I'll be there shortly." He shifted the box of files to create a little space for himself. "What about the list of all the workers, past and present at the farm, has that been completed?"

Jennifer pushed the slider on her typewriter, which jingled before it slammed against the stop. She turned a knurled plastic knob around a few times before pulling out a sheet of paper. "Here it is, sir, I've just finished typing it."

"That's the full list of everyone working at Hinckley Farm?" Ronald sounded surprised. Jennifer ignored him, choosing instead to speak directly to Max.

"As far as I could determine from the payroll records – and the Hinckleys kept very detailed records – the full names and National Registration Card numbers for each employee were all listed in their books. Even the part-time employees were listed. I took the liberty of typing up the list for you on one sheet of paper to make it easier to read."

"Good work, Miss Yumbe." Max looked approvingly at the list of names. Then, turning to the young detective. "Ronald, I want you to start with this ... I need you to run through every name on this list and find out about each of these individuals and where they were on the night of the attack. I want to know if any of them has a history of criminal behaviour or indeed anything suspicious that might be of interest to this case. As we embark on interrogating each farmworker I want to be armed with background information on each one of them. Is that clear?" Ronald nodded. "So, shall I abandon the files for the moment?" Max tightened his lips, then rubbed a hand over his chin. "Well, we can't do everything at once," he said dryly, handing the neatly typed list of names to Ronald.

Then picking up the *Daily Mail* from his desk, he left the office. As he walked down the corridor, he glanced at the headline '*MURDER*

AT HINCKLEY FARM!' Underneath the bold typeface lay the subtext: *'Mr. and Mrs. Hinckley hacked to death by a murderous gang. British government expresses concern over Queen's safety ahead of her visit!'* He folded the newspaper and pinned it under his arm. Such headlines were not going to make his job any easier.

❄

The detective sat in a wooden chair facing Nawakwi, who was visibly distraught. He clasped his fingers underneath his chin, his elbows digging into the worn upholstery of his chair. "I want you to tell me again exactly what you saw yesterday morning. Take me through every detail from the beginning." His voice was calm but firm.

Nawakwi's upper lip began to quiver. "I – I tell you *bwana*, before … before." Max nodded but pressed on. This time switching into Bemba. "*Shimika fyonse ifyo wa mwene mailo,* I need to record a written statement."

They spent about an hour going through each detail. How Nawakwi had woken up about 3:45 in the morning to start her charcoal fire to heat up water for her bucket shower. She described how she had then woken up her two daughters to get them ready for school. Both daughters went to the local village school approximately two kilometres from Hinckley Farm. Nawakwi had prepared breakfast for her children and then, as on every weekday, she had left for the farmhouse at about 4:45 a.m. The walk across the field took her about ten minutes so she would have arrived shortly before 5 a.m., and entered through the back door to the kitchen using her key. She had set the water on the stove to make the morning tea and then proceeded to wash the dishes from the night before. It was only when she entered the dining room that she discovered that someone had broken into the house. Nawakwi had then run to seek help. Her story was essentially the same as the one she had given them the day before.

The memories seemed to stir up raw emotions for Nawakwi. Max waited as she wiped the tears from her eyes. "You knew where the Hinckley's hid their safe and that they kept money inside it, not so?"

Max asked her in Bemba. She nodded timidly. He asked whether she had told anyone about it. Nawakwi shook her head, she had not told anyone.

Then Max asked her about the father of her children. Was he alive, and if so where was he? She told him how she had had a husband once but she had not seen him for close to three years. He had gone to work in the gold mines in Johannesburg and never returned – never even written a letter. It was an oft repeated tale. Men left supposedly to look after their wives and families and disappeared into the big city without a trace. Max took down the name of Nawakwi's husband. His name was Mwalimu. He would have to investigate the man's whereabouts. Many men found their first taste for crime in Jo'burg.

Max wondered briefly what would happen to the young woman, the only breadwinner. Now she had no job, and presumably even her home was in jeopardy, depending on when eventually the farm was sold, or given to the Hinckley's heirs. He couldn't help but feel pity for the young housemaid.

The interview over, Max escorted Nawakwi to a verandah outside the station building to wait for an officer to take her back to the farm after he had spoken with the foreman. Bashi Joshua was ushered into the interrogation room. He seemed poised but eager to be done with it all. Max would spend another hour and half taking down a written statement. Bashi Joshua's account of the previous days' events was again consistent with what he had told the officers initially. Max asked the foreman if he had known about the safe or any valuables that may have been kept inside it. The sturdy farm supervisor shook his head saying that it was well known by all the farmworkers that Elijah the driver was responsible for taking the Hinckley's money into town every so often, but nobody working outside of the house would have known about a safe nor where it was hidden. Max probed, trying to find out if there was anyone the supervisor knew who could have wished the Hinckleys harm. It was clear he didn't know of anybody. The Hinckleys were well loved and respected by all the workers. Satisfied with the foreman's answers, Max let him go to join Nawakwi, so they could both be taken back to the farm.

Next on Max's list of things to do was to collect a formal statement from Elijah, the driver. The statements recorded by the Makeni police where riddled with grammatical errors and barely legible. It had been a good decision to transfer Elijah to HQ so that he could do it properly. When he was brought into the interrogation room, he looked to be in a much better condition than when he had last seen him. "I trust you were treated well here at Central?" Max began.

Elijah nodded. "Yes sir, thank you sir." There was relief in his voice.

"Do you know why I had you transferred here?" Max asked.

Elijah hesitated. His lips moved as if to speak but then he drew back into his chair.

Max continued. "My sole interest is to apprehend those who perpetrated this murder, including anyone who aided the killers. I'm a man of the law and I take my responsibilities very seriously, you understand?" Elijah nodded. "You need to tell me the truth about what you know because if I find out you've been lying to me – and believe me I will – it will be very bad for you." He looked directly at Elijah. "I need you to think very carefully and start by telling me exactly where you were in the early hours of Friday, July 20th…"

When Max finally walked upstairs and back to his office, he sank into his chair. The interrogations had gone much as he had expected. In his estimation neither the foreman, the housemaid nor the driver had anything to with the crime. It was too early to completely rule them out but he was fairly certain about their innocence.

They would have to wait on results on the vehicle registration which he expected he would be receiving later in the day. Perhaps that would yield some new leads. In the meantime, he would spend some time going through the box of files, still sitting on top of his desk. He reached into it and pulled out a folder but before he could open it, Ronald spoke up.

"Boss, I think we may have something!" There was excitement in his voice. "I was going through the list of names but not coming up with anything, so I thought of another approach and I think I may have stumbled upon something of interest."

"Go on …"

"I had the idea to place calls to all the prisons within the province to see if any one of the workers spent some time there – the prisons always keep good records of all their inmates. To narrow down the search, I asked them to look at their records over the past year. So far, none of the workers on this list showed up." But, Ronald held up the typed leaf of paper in his hand, a satisfied grin on his face. "But … the farm foreman had given us a list of casuals, vendors, and so on. " He reached for his small ring-bound notepad and glanced over at Jennifer who pretended to be busy on her typewriter. "Two of the names on the foreman's list are employees of a milling company that supplies them with stock feed twice a week … it's called Ifundo Milling Limited." Revelling in the moment, Ronald straightened his back to deliver his punchline. "I called them up and asked a few questions. They confirmed that the same two people make the twice weekly deliveries to Hinckley Farm. They've been working there for several years … however, the company recently hired a new chap … Paul Mutamina … he joined about three months ago. Apparently he was on training shortly after he was hired and accompanied the old hands in making deliveries to Hinckley Farm. However, several weeks ago he suddenly stopped reporting for work." Max raised an eyebrow. "They were quite upset about it. They say he just simply disappeared without warning or explanation, *kaya* … just like that. So I looked him up … turns out he's an ex-convict … spent a couple of years in Chimutengo Prison for attempted robbery and was released just eight months ago. It appears he lied on his application form when they hired him at Ifundo. I can't be sure boss, but he could very well have something to do with this crime."

Max leant forward in his chair, this was certainly valuable investigative police work. Ronald had the potential to be a good detective if only he would improve his bedside manner. "We need to find this chap and bring him into the station for questioning at once." Max declared. "Find where he lives and send an officer out to bring him in!"

✳

Max frowned and rubbed his chin before placing both elbows on his desk. "Nobody has seen this fellow for the past three days?"

Ronald shook his head. "No sir. No one has seen or heard from him. We sent two local officers to the address on his employment files in Kafue Township. They've just telephoned to say that he wasn't there … apparently, he has disappeared. He has a wife and two small children and in the past few weeks, nobody has seen them either. I think he's definitely a person of interest, something doesn't smell quite right."

Max stood for a moment. "You're quite possibly onto something. We need to find him soon." He rubbed his chin once more as his mind flicked through his options like a deck of cards. "We need to go back to his township."

"But two officers from Kafue outpost were just out there and didn't find anything …"

Max checked the time on his wrist. It was 4:09 p.m. If they left now, they could still make it to Kafue before dark. "I want to go out there myself." His tone spelt finality. "If this chap was part of something big enough to make sure he moved his family ahead of time, then somebody somewhere must have seen or heard something. People talk, it's their nature, they just can't help it."

45

8

The Dutchman

Mukushi District, approximately three hundred kilometres north of Lusaka

Frits stared at the telegram. A narrow slip of paper with one line typed across it:

"Lawyers contacted. Formal summons to follow."

Slowly, he removed his spectacles. He'd been expecting the message, but that didn't make it any easier. The woman behind the counter of the local store, which doubled as the post office, waited in silence. She recognised the rugged man, who came in every two weeks for groceries, but she'd never seen him so clearly unnerved.

"Is this all? … Is there anything else for me?" he asked.

The woman shook her head. "No *bwana*, only that one *sah*, that's the only message. It came early this morning."

Frits rubbed his eyes with the back of his hand before replacing his heavy glasses, and shook his head as if to clear his mind, suddenly noticing the headline on the pile of newspapers to his left: *"MURDER AT HINCKLEY FARM!"* Shocked, he involuntarily stepped backwards while searching in his pockets for coins, 'I'll take a copy, please," he said, picking up the newspaper and moving away from the counter to the relief of the sales assistant.

Hurriedly, unfolding the tabloid, he scanned the first few lines:

"Well known white couple Laura and Henry Hinckley hacked to death on their

farm during early hours of Friday morning. Lusaka Central Police investigating'.

"Christ!" Frits exclaimed, "I need to use your phone."

The woman frowned. "The phone is for workers only." She looked down at her watch, "… and we close at sixteen hours, I can't just let …"

"Yes, yes, I know …" Frits interrupted, "… but this is important, very important … these… these people …" He pointed at the newspaper. "I know these people … they're my friends… they've been murdered. I need to call Lusaka Central Police right away, do you understand?"

The woman pushed her seat back, the legs of the chair scraping against the floor. "Wait one moment… I must first check with my boss." She lifted herself heavily from her seat and made her way to the back room.

As Frits waited, he ran his fingers nervously over a set of dirt-stained divots on the counter. Surely, it couldn't be true. How had Laura and Henry been killed? What had happened? What went wrong? Tears welled in his eyes, and he hastily blinked them back. Men don't cry.

He stared up at the obligatory framed photograph of President Kenneth Kaunda, a sarong flung over his left shoulder. The young president sat proudly, his gaze enigmatically focused on a point in the distance. A youthful leader emblematic of a new Africa in which its indigenous people were in charge of their destiny. How things had changed since Frits first arrived in what was then Northern Rhodesia. How starkly his fortunes had plummeted since Independence. He could remember as if it were yesterday when the British ruled supreme and Africans were subservient to white men like him.

❉

1956

Copperbelt Province, Northern Rhodesia

He arrived on the Copperbelt from the gold mines of Johannesburg during the time of the Federation when Northern and Southern

Rhodesia were coupled with Nyasaland under British colonial rule. Like many young white men at the time, he was lured to Rhodesia by the prospect of striking it rich in the burgeoning mineral prospecting industry. Unlike South Africa, Northern Rhodesia's gemstone industry was still largely untapped and so he'd taken the gamble to travel hundreds of miles north. Frits had dreamed of finding emeralds, gold, and even perhaps diamonds.

Soon afterwards, in February 1957, Frits met a young Englishman by the name of Henry Hinckley. Both were in their early twenties, unmarried and with a proclivity for adventure. Although they were both white men in Africa, their views about indigenous African people could not have been more different. Henry, having grown up in England, tended to view Africans with a level of empathy, although unable to fully acknowledge them as his equal.

As a boy Henry had spent several of his school holidays visiting his wealthy uncle, Rab Butler, in Knightsbridge, London. Rab was a rising politician who would in later years serve in the British cabinet. In those days his uncle employed an elderly black housemaid called Betsy, who was originally from Jamaica. Henry remembered delicious pies and how, when he was very small, she would tuck him into bed and weave mysterious tales of her ancestors who came from somewhere deep in the heart of the African continent. When Betsy died, Henry was in ninth grade at Plymouth Grammar School in Lancashire, and he'd run into the woods sobbing bitterly, hoping that none of his mates would see him. He had vowed then to go to Africa and visit the home of Betsy's ancestors. Frits had no such fondness for black people. Things were very clear in his mind: whites were superior to blacks. Having been born and raised on a farm in South Africa, Frits had no qualms about putting the black African in his rightful place.

In those early years, Frits and Henry worked together in a small prospecting company named Chesterman and Oakley, founded in the late nineteenth century by two Englishmen. The two young men had viewed each other with suspicion and youthful rivalry as their teams of ten or so men would be sent into the bush in search of mineral deposits, sleeping in the open air for weeks on end. It was a Spartan life, but Frits and Henry proved resilient – both men suffered incidences of malaria and Frits once nearly died from yellow fever that incapacitated him for close to a month. It was during those times that the two men developed a friendship.

In 1958, upon the request of his uncle, Henry left Northern Rhodesia to return to London where he would spend the next fourteen months. Concerned about his nephew's future, Rab Butler had arranged for Henry to begin a respectable career in the civil service. The young man had given it a go for several months but sitting at a desk in a crammed office in the north of England, he found himself longing to return to the warmth, the clean air and the golden sunsets of Africa. He would do so in 1959 but this time with a wife by his side, a red-headed firebrand called Laura.

❈

The woman reappeared, "You can come this side," she said pointing to a door to her left.

Lusaka Central Police Station

What happened? Had something gone wrong? Why had the murders been so brutal? Jennifer Yumbe had not been able to stop thinking about the killings at Hinckley Farm. She'd been working at the police station for over a year now, and had discovered that police work really interested her, but never had she heard of anything like this. 'They might have been killing mad pigs," she thought. Why? Zambians were not brutal people. Yes, there'd been other murders. Usually domestic, often because a man had had too much to drink... she shook her head, as if trying to clear it. The telephone on Detective Max Chanda's desk rang suddenly and she was grateful to have her train of thought broken.

"Hullo? Special Crimes Unit, Detective Maxwell Chanda's office. May I assist you?" There was a short pause before the operator spoke, he sounded distracted.

"Can I speak to Detective Chanda."

"No, I'm afraid he's just left the office. May I take a message?"

"I've a caller who needs to speak to him. He says it's urgent. I think it's about the Hinckley case…"

Jennifer knew the switchboard operator. A young man who was easily stressed. She often wondered why he had come to work at a police station, and why they had accepted him.

"I'm sorry, you've just missed him." She said, firmly. "Please put him through, I can take a message?"

She heard a shuffling sound for a few seconds followed by the crackle of static. Eventually she heard a man's voice. She recognised the accent immediately, it was a white man, most likely a Boer from South Africa.

He asked. "Is this the detective in charge of the case in the paper? The one about Hinckley Farm?"

"No sir, this is Detective Maxwell Chanda's secretary… he's not in the office at the moment but I can give him a message as soon as he gets back."

"No, no, no, I need to speak to your *bwana*. Don't you understand?"

Jennifer attempted to speak again but he cut her off. "Tell him I'll see him tomorrow morning. I'm leaving for Lusaka right away!"

"Your name sir…? I didn't get your name."

"Frits … Frits Hubercht, friend to Laura and Henry Hinckley." With that, the line went dead.

9

Following the Breadcrumbs

5:26 p.m.

Kafue Township – fifty kilometres south of Lusaka

A young uniformed police officer by the name of Samuel Mando sat squeezed between Max and Ronald in the front of the police van. The two detectives had arrived at Kafue police outpost shortly before 5:00 p.m. and had insisted on taking Samuel with them to lead them to Paul Mutamina's last recorded place of residence. It was Samuel, under instruction from HQ, who had gone out into the township earlier in the day in search of him.

Kafue Township was a settlement of ramshackle dwellings that covered the landscape like mushrooms budding over a hillside. Samuel pointed his finger in the direction of a maze of tightly packed homes. "*Apo!*" he announced as Max steered the vehicle along a dusty track. Ronald scanned the area in front of them. It was difficult to tell the single room structures apart. "Are you sure?" He asked the young officer.

"Yes *sah*, it's the one." Samuel confirmed. It was dusk and the setting sun was beginning to cast a gentle orange hue over the township. Max drew closer and parked the vehicle a few yards from a cluster of homes. A group of ashen-faced children momentarily halted their game of football to stare in curiosity at the three men disembarking from the beige Land Rover.

Samuel led the way towards two women standing in front of the cluster of homes a short distance away. One of them had a child strapped in a *chitenge* over her back, the other was poised above a charcoal brazier with a wooden ladle resting across the top of a fire stained pot. "*Chungulopo mukwai*" Samuel greeted them. The two women genuflected, each one clapping her palms together gently in deference to the three authority figures before them.

The woman with the child lowered her eyes "*Mwaisenipo mukwai*," she greeted them.

Samuel introduced the two detectives at his side and explained that the men had come to ask more questions about Paul Mutamina and his family. The woman stole a nervous glance at the two detectives before dropping her eyes again, the crusty nosed child on her back remained still with its eyes full of sleep.

Max led with his questions in Bemba. He asked her which house Mutamina and his family lived in. The woman pointed out a small structure to her left with a rusted corrugated metal roofing sheet for a door. She explained that Paul Mutamina and his wife, Judy, had a small child and they lived in the home next to hers. She was friends with his wife and their children often played together in the compound. Max asked when she had last seen them. As if on cue, the child on her back shifted restlessly. She leaned forward and adjusted the knot in her *chitenge*, then began to rock the child slowly from right to left to soothe him back to sleep. Ronald repeated Max's unanswered question, this time with a stern warning for the woman to tell the truth or else she would find herself in a lot of trouble. She said it had been over a week since Judy and her child had left to go to their village in Lundazi District to visit her relatives. As for Paul, he hadn't been seen in several days. Max pressed her to be more specific but she repeated that she was not sure – three maybe four days? Max knew that he would have to send word to officers in Lundazi District to search for Mutamina's wife and family.

"And your husband? Where's your husband? Is he friends with Mutamina?" Ronald went on to ask but the woman shook her head. She was a widow with three children. She said that she hardly spoke to Paul; she only spoke to his wife. The couple had not lived long in the area. All she knew of the man was that he would always leave home before dawn to join other labourers on the main road trying to hitch a ride on one of the trucks that collected produce from commercial farms in the Makeni area.

Max asked the woman about how it was possible for Mutamina and his entire family to just disappear without anyone knowing. They must have said something to somebody. Again, the woman shook her head. All she had known was that Judy had left to visit her relatives in the village and she only realised that something was wrong when two police officers arrived asking questions.

The detectives went on for several more minutes taking down names and notes. Finally, Max asked if she knew the name of the person who owned the house in which the Mutamina family lived. The woman explained that the same landlord owned many of the small homes in the area, his name was Lucas Nzima, and he also owned a popular tavern in the township called Nsunga Bar. On most evenings one could usually find him there. Officer Samuel acknowledged that he knew the tavern and its owner. Max scribbled the name into his notepad and placed it back into his shirt pocket. He turned to Sam and asked. "Did you search the home?"

Sam nodded. "Yes *sah*, but we didn't find anything *sah*... just some clothes and a few pots... that's all."

Max rubbed his chin. He smelled a rat. He eyed the small dwelling ahead of him. He decided to see the landlord in case he had any more details about his tenant that could prove useful in locating Mutamina's whereabouts, but first he decided to look inside the small house himself.

The door opened into a room. It jutted against the floor sending specks of dust into the evening air. It was a small windowless dwelling illuminated only by the light from the open door. Max entered followed closely behind by Ronald, Samuel remained outside. There was a musty smell in the room, no doubt from too many bodies sleeping in a single space. A reed mat, a pair of trousers and a threadbare shirt lay on the floor in an untidy pile. Max picked up the trousers and searched the contents of the pockets – they were empty.

"There's not much here." Ronald stated the obvious. Max straightened himself and looked around. In the corner behind him and to the left of the door was a small set of metallic dishes – a few cups, pots and plates and some plastic containers. The plates were crusted over with what looked like the remnants of old food. Max rubbed his chin. It seemed to him that the woman outside was telling the truth about the departure of Mutamina's wife, for no woman would leave her home in this state.

"What do you think boss? Where to next?" Ronald asked.

Max's eyes searched the room once more. "I want to talk to the landlord, Lucas Nzima, I want to hear what he has to say about our chap Mutamina."

Tawdry magazine cut-outs of scantily clad women lined the walls of Nsunga Bar. The night was young but the place was already teeming with men of all ages slugging cheap alcohol. There was a certain headiness in the way they drank, it was as if the bartender had announced that his stock was running low. Snippets of conversations filled the air – grievances about work or the lack thereof, marital woes, sports and politics were all being discussed at once, forming one unintelligible din. Max, Ronald and Samuel scanned the smoke-filled room for a few seconds before settling on some short wooden stools near the back exit. It was not so unpleasant at the back as a warm breeze came through the open door. Samuel seemed very at home in the environment, as the bar was scarcely three kilometres from his home. Officer Samuel grinned when Max asked him what he wanted to drink. "*Ka Mosi mwemfumu*," he responded eagerly. At Max's signal a diminutive barman made his way to take their order.

"Is it always this full?" Ronald asked.

Samuel smiled broadly. "*Ni pa* weekend *chabe!* Every weekend and *pa* month end *ni* worse! *Chilalila mwemfumu!*" He dipped his head and began to sway his body to a song that had just been turned up on a speaker.

"Is Nzima here? Have you seen him?" Max asked, straining to be heard above the din.

Samuel shook his head. "No, *sah*. Not yet, but it's early, I'm sure he'll be here now-now."

Ronald asked a question but Max shook his head. "What? I didn't hear you." The two men leaned forward. Ronald was now shouting into Max's ear. "I said… I'm sure somebody here must have known Mutamina."

Max nodded.

The barman returned holding three brown bottles, and handed one to each of them. Max dug into his back pocket and pulled out his wallet. "Keep them coming, I'll pay you for the rest afterwards."

Samuel took a swig and swallowed. "Ah *ni* best!" He raised his thumb in the air.

Max and Ronald had their eyes fixed on everyone entering and leaving the establishment. After almost an hour, Samuel leaned towards Max. "That's him *sah*, *ba* Lucas Nzima." A short well-groomed man stood talking to one of the bartenders behind the counter. Max gave a signal to Ronald and the two detectives rose from their stools.

Once Max and Ronald had introduced themselves to Lucas Nzima, he cordially ushered them into a back room where they could talk, closing the door behind them. Much quieter, the back room was also a storage area: red plastic beer crates were stacked against each of the walls. "So, how can I assist you?" Lucas asked, his arms over his chest. As far as Max could tell, the man seemed unintimidated at the prospect of speaking with two detectives from the city.

"We're investigating a case, a very sensitive case, and we're trying to locate one of your former tenants to answer a few questions. His name is Paul Mutamina. Do you know where we can find him?"

Lucas Nzima pursed his lips. "Ah yes … that scoundrel. I know him very well, detective. I too am looking for him. He has run off with my money, disappeared just like that without paying his rent!" Lucas squeezed his jaw. "He asked me to give him more time … said he'd just started work at a local milling company and had to pay for his sick child to go to hospital. I felt sorry for him, I let him stay for two months while he sorted himself out … two months! Then he upped and disappeared… it was all a pack of lies! Two months' rent, that's what that scoundrel owes me!"

"Any idea at all where he could have run off to?" Ronald asked.

Lucas raised a finger in front of his face. "If I knew that, detective, you would be arresting me for killing the bastard!"

"What about any friends, acquaintances of his, do you know anybody who might know where he could be?" Lucas shook his head before sounding off again about the money he was owed.

Max and Ronald soon returned into the bar to find Samuel chatting with a neighbour. Max signalled to the barman that he wanted to pay, and pulling out his wallet removed some crumpled bank notes and began to count them. As he did so, he paused, asking. "Do you know a man by the name of Paul Mutamina?" There was a flash of unease across the barman's face, he instantly averted his eyes. Max repeated his question.

The barman swallowed hard. "*Sah… sah…*"

"*Iwe*, I asked you a question."

"… *Sah* … he comes here but … *sah* … I haven't seen him for some time, *sah.*"

The barman's dithering annoyed Ronald sitting next to Maxwell. "*Iwe tuli ma* detectives from Lusaka Central. We are doing a very serious investigation, we need to locate him. Do you know where he is? *Kamba che* what you know or else *uzayenda kuma* cells, we'll lock you up *manje so!*"

The little man's upper lip began to tremble. "*Sah*, I don't know anything, *sah*. I swear to you *sah* I don't know anything…"

Ronald stood up, he towered over the diminutive man. "*Iwe* this is not a joking matter. We're doing a serious investigation. We'll take you *ku* station and you'll be sleeping *muma* cells *chabe* … in fact let's go *manje so*, now – now, *kamani!*"

The man pleaded. "*Ba* boss *napapata*, please … I …I …" But before he could say any more Ronald had grabbed him by the arm and began pulling him towards the door. Few of the other customers noticed what was going on. Max and Samuel followed.

The barman fell to his knees. "*Sah*, please, please, *napapata* … Mutamina is not a friend of mine. I only serve him as a customer. He comes here sometimes, but I haven't seen him … that's all I know. I … I swear to you."

Max felt uneasy about Ronald's rough treatment of the man, though he also felt that the barman was hiding something. Fear was ambivalent. Max recalled his conversation with Chief Mbewe at the station and the pompous British foreign officer who had rankled him so much. Time was of the essence in this case, and so far, they had not pieced together who had killed the Hinckleys and why.

Ronald slapped the barman's face.

"*Napapata, napapata* boss …" he cried out, lifting his arms to protect himself.

"Enough of that!" Max raised his voice. "There's no need for violence. Let the man speak." He stepped forward as Ronald took a step back, clenching his fists. Max now hovered above the little man who was still shielding his face. "Tell us what you know about Paul Mutamina. Hurry up! We need to know everything you know. Do you understand?"

After several deep breaths, the barman gathered himself together. "He … he talked about a job …"

Max nodded. "Go on."

The barman continued. "He … he came into the bar about three, maybe four weeks ago with a lot of money … cash … he -he was boasting about finding a job that would make him a very rich man … make him rich like *ba bolokwa mu ma yadi ku* Lusaka. He said the money was an advance he was given for starting a new job. You must believe me *sah*, that's all I heard … that's all I know."

"What job did he say it was and where?" Max asked.

The barman shook his head. "I-I don't know *sah*… I swear to you, that's all I know, that's all he said about it."

Max eyed the frightened little man. "And how do we know you're telling the truth, eh? … For all we know you and him are working together!"

"No *sah*, no *sah* ... I swear ..." The barman choked on his words.

Max paused for a moment. "But why didn't you tell us this when I asked you about him?"

The man shook his head in resignation. "I... I was afraid *sah* ... I... I was afraid."

"Afraid of what?" Ronald shouted. The man flinched at the sound of Ronald's voice.

"I was afraid of getting fired ... my ... my *bwana* is looking for him. Mutamina owes him a lot of money. If my *bwana* finds out that I have anything to do with Mutamina ..." He gave a huge sigh. "That will be the end of me."

Max thought the barman was telling the truth but he knew that he had no choice but to take him into HQ for further questioning. He did, however, feel pity for the man for he realised that the barman would almost certainly lose his job.

As they drove back to the city, Max peered through the windshield of his car into the distance. All around them was darkness on either side of the road. Every so often, bright headlamps would zoom past them in the opposite lane like shooting stars in the night sky. The two detectives sat silently next to each other, each man with his thoughts. Max began to replay the events of the past two days: Mr and Mrs Hinckley bludgeoned to death by a band of criminals who were still at large. A suspect, the driver, who Max was certain had nothing to do with the crime. Then there were the housemaid and the foreman who had discovered the bodies. Again, he was fairly certain that they were innocent. He had his suspicions about the housemaid's estranged husband who she claimed she had not seen in years. Could she be lying about not having been in contact with him and perhaps told him about the Hinckley's safe? It was possible but not plausible. So far, the biggest lead they had was Paul Mutamina. Max did not know if he had anything to do with the killings but his previous conviction for robbery and his sudden disappearance did raise questions.

A large freight truck blasting its full beams made Max avert his eyes, he reduced speed until it had passed them. He remembered his conversation with Chief Mbewe and the British foreign officer. Max felt a renewed surge of irritation, it was hard enough to solve a murder case without having to contend with political interference. This pressure to solve the case and wrap everything up neatly before the Queen's arrival in a few days' time. He thought about the two boxes of documents waiting for them at the office. They would need to spend part of the night going through them to see if there was anything useful for the case. There was no time to waste. Max also hoped that Jennifer had managed to schedule an appointment with the warden at Chimutengo Prison. They would need to find out more about Paul Mutamina and his time in the prison, perhaps that would help them locate him. He would also have to send word to officers in Lundazi District to search for Mutamina's wife and family.

For now, at least, finding Paul Mutamina was critical. However, what they would learn in the hours to come was that all roads would lead to a man by the name of Amos Kapambwe Mushili, a cold calculating figure whose resolve knew no bounds.

10

The Story of Amos Kapambwe Mushili

Friday, 25th April 1975

Four years prior to the attack on Hinckley Farm ...

Amos Mushili ran his fingers down the left side of the woman's face, down her neck and all the way to the top of her cleavage. She smiled playfully, cocking her neck back. "So, you haven't told me your name," he said.

"And why do you wanna know?" The woman, who wore red lipstick and large earrings which winked in the light, replied.

"Is it wrong for a man to ask for a woman's name?" He asked feigning amazement. The sound of a live jazz band played softly in the background. Amos and the young woman sat on tall wooden stools facing each other at the poolside bar. Friday evenings at the Pamodzi Hotel always seemed to draw a handsome crowd of revellers, many of them British and American expats. The son of a Judge, Amos mingled in these circles. The young woman shook her head and extended her slender finger to touch the tip of his nose.

"Uh-uh" she smiled.

"... That's not good enough. You'll have to do better than that." Amos had played this game many times before, and knew the dance of courtship, as did she.

"Won't you give me a hint?"

She took a sip of her cocktail. "... and what's in it for me?"

"Hmmm let's see ... If I guess three times and get it wrong, I'll buy you another drink?"

"And if you get it right…?"

He smiled mischievously, his eyes dropping to her low-cut blouse.

She paused, taking another sip, "… Well… it's the name of a flower."

Amos protested, "That's not much of a clue is it? There're thousands of flowers…."

"Hey, you chose the rules!" She raised an eyebrow in stern admonition.

Amos gave a small smile of agreement as he approvingly assessed his prize. Chiselled features, high cheek bones, a long neck and eyes that betrayed her smile. "Hmmm… let me see… Rrrr … Rose?"

The woman shook her head slowly.

"Lilly?"

Another shake of the head.

She picked up her cocktail glass and raised it towards her lips. "You have one more chance… make it count."

Amos narrowed his eyes. "Hmmm… Violet?" The woman dropped her gaze observing a little manly chest-hair peeking above his unbuttoned shirt and then slowly raised her eyes to meet his.

He collected a set of keys from the concierge, two small silver keys attached to a wooden fob with the room number marked on it. She stood a distance away near an elevator in the lobby. She had a small purse pinned underneath her elbow. Her platform shoes made her appear taller than her five-foot frame, a miniskirt revealing her toned legs. The young attendant wearing a blazer behind the counter could not resist a smirk as he gave the room keys to Amos.

Amos discretely brushed the outside of his hand against her leg as they waited for the elevator to descend. Their room was on the tenth floor, and as they stood in silence, they sensed the disapproval of the older couple sharing the elevator with them. Leaving the lift, they walked along the carpeted corridor to their room. Amos fumbled with the keys, dropping them to the floor and picking them up again before turning the lock. The room was of a decent size, with a small television set on a wooden table, a love seat with green upholstery to the side. In the centre of the room was a neatly made queen-sized bed.

Amos circled his arm around her waist and pulled her towards him but she wriggled her way from his clutches. "Uh-uh," Violet wagged a finger in his face. "You know how it goes… Pay first." She held out her hand. Amos reached into his back pocket and pulled out his wallet. He counted several crisp bank notes and laid them in her open palm. Even though she had watched him count the money, she thumbed through it again, to make sure. Then she stuffed the notes deep inside her purse.

She fastened her brassiere from the front before rotating it until it was the right way around. The elastic straps slapped against her skin as she pulled them over her shoulders. Still lying in bed, Amos watched her getting dressed.

"That was truly amazing," he said rubbing his chest. The son of a renowned judge, he had grown up in comfortable surroundings. Amos' father had been one of a few black law clerks under colonial rule. After Independence, he became a lawyer and then a judge, ultimately rising to the position of Chief Justice. On account of his father, Amos attended the most prestigious schools in the country – Munali Boys and later Saint Paul's Boarding School. His father then found him a place at Evelyn Hone College in the capital; later, again through his father's connections, Amos was employed as a junior manager at a government-owned supermarket in the centre of town. But despite – or perhaps because of – his privileged upbringing, Amos had a restless soul. The lure of a fast life always proved irresistible.

Violet glanced over her shoulder and smiled. Amos extended his arm and began to stroke her, running his fingers down to the small of her back. "Must you leave so quickly?"

Without turning to look at him, she laughed. "You know the deal, sweetie. You have to pay double if you want me to stay longer."

"Ah come on, baby, you know I'm good for it, eh? Why *unichaya* so?"

Ignoring his plea, she rose to her feet and slipped on her top. She had her back to him as she began to fix the buttons on her blouse. Amos shifted towards her and reached for her arm. His grip was tight around her forearm. She attempted to pull away but he held on to her.

"Let go of me." She turned to face him.

Still gripping her arm, he sat up, irritated. "Stop playing hard to get."

She smacked his hand once, quick and hard, her rings like knuckledusters and stepped away, "I have to go." She reached for her purse on the night stand and turned to leave. Amos rose up from the bed and blocked her path. "I'm not finished with you."

He towered over her but she was not afraid of him, in her line of work she had been in a scrap or two. "Get out of my way, I'm warning you!"

"*Atase iwe!* Who do you think you're talking to, eh? I'll tell you when you can leave!" Amos leaned into her, his face now inches from hers. She made another attempt to get past him but it was thwarted. Cornered, she swiped at him. Startled, Amos staggered back and touched his face – she had drawn blood. He saw red.

One blow is all it took. He slammed her head against a footstool and she lay motionless on the carpeted floor.

The magistrate sentenced him to seven years with hard labour at Chimutengo Prison for voluntary manslaughter. His parents would not attend the sentencing – he had brought unimaginable shame and suffering on his family and they had shed many tears.

But as Amos was led in shackles to an open van ferrying the latest cohort of prisoners to Chimutengo, he showed no remorse. Violet had left him with a permanent reminder in the form of a conspicuous scar on his left cheek. Scarification that would only serve to bolster the image that he would expertly cultivate in prison as one to be feared. And as happens all too often, prison proved a criminal rite of passage. Amos left more hardened and ruthless than he had gone in.

❋

Paul Mutamina and Amos Mushili were first acquainted when the two men sat next to each other on the dusty corrugated floor of an open van taking them from the courthouse to prison. There were fifteen men in total, all shackled and huddled together on the bumpy two and a half hour ride out of the city. Orange dust rose from the earth as the vehicle made its way along a gravel track. Paul was twenty-two years old at the time, and he and his wife Judy had a two-year-old daughter. With Paul on his way to prison, his young family were now facing the prospect of the next five years without an income. Earlier that day, Judy had sat on a wooden pew in the back of a packed courtroom trying her best to make sense of what was being said. It had taken all of four months for Paul Mutamina to have his day in court. For four months, he had been remanded in a dingy police cell that smelled of human excrement. When the day finally came for the robbery case to be heard in front of a magistrate, Paul was brought in with several others all looking dishevelled and resigned to their fate. The proceedings lasted no longer than twenty minutes. Judy watched anxiously as a man wearing a curly white wig, too small for his head, read from a single sheet of paper before slamming what looked like a hammer onto his high table. As they led Paul away into the back of the courtroom, Judy panicked asking the people around her to explain what had just transpired. That was when she was told that her husband had been sentenced to five years with hard labour. She had instinctively tightened her embrace of the child nestled in her lap before issuing a guttural cry.

Paul had been convicted for participating in a burglary. Anyone who knew Paul could tell that he was not the sharpest tool in the shed, but what he lacked in smarts, he compensated for with his fists. He was a simple carpenter's son who perhaps was guiltier of being gullible than anything else. He had been persuaded by three of his childhood friends to help them break into a house in Kabulonga, one of the leafy suburbs of Lusaka. The whole thing had been a grand failure. It had been a gross miscalculation to break into a house just three streets away from a police station. An officer had walked past the house and spotted a couple of empty sacks hanging over a wall. This was a well know tactic used by thieves. The sacks provided protection from the shards of glass cemented into the wall, so they could easily be mounted. The police officer had quickly gathered reinforcements and soon the jig was up. All four men had been apprehended while still inside the property and now their respective families were to pay dearly for the ill-fated attempt at larceny.

If there was one thing Amos knew how to do well, it was to spot weaknesses in people, knowing who he could use and control for his selfish ends. Amos could tell at once that Paul was someone he could manipulate. When they arrived at the prison, the men were told to disembark from the back of the van. A stern-faced guard in a starched uniform barked instructions. He told them to line up in a single file. Amos noticed Paul's trembling hands as they shuffled to take their positions, one behind the other. Amos knew that his mettle would be tested in prison, it was not a matter of *if* but *when*. He would certainly prove himself worthy of the respect of his fellow inmates and a set of serendipitous events would help ensure that he would be elevated to near mythical status in prison lore.

When all fifteen men had been lined up, they were promptly marched down to a small building inside the perimeter fence. The ageing structure had a rusted metal roof and pale blue paint peeling off its walls. They stood at attention as one by one they were ushered inside to stand in front of a registration desk. A woman in uniform entered their names into a thick log book. Their national registration cards and any personal effects were collected and taken into a back room for safe keeping. None of the inmates held any hope that their belongings would ever be returned. Next the men were marched past the open courtyard towards an ablution block that stood several yards behind the main prison building. An open gutter ran the length of the old decrepit building. Here they were told to strip naked while four prison guards, three of them wielding batons, took turns at inspecting each man. One after another each inmate would open his mouth spit out his tongue. Arms were raised, legs spread apart, buttocks and nether regions examined. The guards seemed to derive pleasure in the whole affair, it appeared designed to humiliate and firmly establish who was in charge. Two of the men were handed buckets and directed to draw water from a nearby tap. A long bar of cheap soap was thrust into their hands. The men huddled together around the two buckets and lathered themselves while the guards yelled for them to hurry up. When the bucket bath was over, each inmate was provided with a pair of khaki shorts and a shirt. They were then promptly marched, single file, into the maize field to join the other prisoners. They would work in the field until sunset.

When it was time to head back to the prison cells, one of the guards blew his whistle. All of the old inmates knew the drill, they immediately formed a line holding their hoes and slashers at their sides. Seeing this, the new prisoners followed suit and stood in line. It was at that moment when one of the seasoned inmates snickered at Amos. "You won't last in here with those soft hands," he said. "In here those hands are only good for one thing – *wala cimona lelo* – tonight you'll see things!" Clutching his crotch he blew a kiss at Amos. This sent several of the inmates who were within earshot cackling like school boys. One of the guards issued a stern warning which instantly restored order. Amos understood the situation very well – to the less astute, this was nothing but a benign taunt, one to be brushed aside, but he knew better. He knew it was a test, one in which he was determined to prove himself. He knew that if he did not show strength in that moment, it would define his entire experience in prison. He circled his fingers around the neck of his hoe and leapt forward.

It took two guards to prize him off the other prisoner. The man was left bleeding with a hoe lodged in his left collar bone. The guards clattered Amos with their batons, laying into him with overwhelming force. And, this is where the story of Amos Mushili takes a bizarre almost mystical turn. Some of the events which followed may in part be apocryphal, but they have been firmly planted in prison lore. It is said that as the guards beat him to within inches of his life, Amos yelled to the heavens and cursed them. They say that he invoked spirits from the netherworld casting a hex on the two guards. It is said that he swore that none of their children would live to see old age and as he spoke these words, a flock of crows fluttered in the trees above. At the same time a snake bit a goat tied to a tree in the field and darkness covered the sky as the moon shielded the setting sun. An ageing inmate lamented that Amos was an evil man who must have made a pact with the devil himself, for how could the words of a man shake the world in such a manner?

Amos was left unconscious and that night he was dragged and thrust into an abandoned dog kennel where he would spend the next several weeks. The kennel was so small that he could not stand up and the corrugated metal roofing panels would leave him baking in the punishing afternoon heat. In one sense the punishment would be worth it for in the following few weeks, a chain of inexplicable events would work in his favour.

The first was the sudden death of one of the two guards' sons. The boy fell sick with a fever the night of the incident in the field. He was rushed to see the prison nurse but died the following morning. The nurse said it was meningitis but the boy's father could not help but remember Amos Mushili's prophetic words. The next strange occurrence was exactly a week later. This time the other guard's wife delivered a stillborn child, the baby would have been her first. After this sad loss, both guards became afraid to go near Amos and two new guards were assigned to his charge. The final straw came when the first guard, the one who had only just buried one of his sons, lost another in a tragic accident. The boy was hit by a car on his way back from school – he died instantly. When news of this latest tragedy filtered through the prison, there were whispers that Amos possessed supernatural powers which he could summon to devastating effect. Prison guards and inmates alike were frightened of him.

Amos Mushili was an educated man who had grown up in an

upper-class suburb of the city. This made him different from most of the inmates at Chimutengo, the majority of whom were illiterate with little to no schooling. He was able to capitalise on their lack of education to fan the rumours of his so-called powers and very soon Mushili had created his own fiefdom within the gates of Chimutengo Prison.

Amos was steadily becoming a law unto himself – ordering fellow inmates to do his bidding. Cigarettes, alcohol and even young village girls would be delivered to him while the guards looked the other way. Fellow inmates would get their wives to prepare meals for him and deliver them into the prison. When Warden Boniface Bwembya, a God-fearing man, caught wind of what was happening in his prison, he was incensed. He decreed that Mushili be separated from the general population and placed into the old chicken run which had been converted into a holding cell. This did little to arrest the situation, in fact it exacerbated it as he now became an inmate set apart from the others. His fellow prisoners would talk amongst themselves about how even the Warden had seen it fit to treat him differently.

11

Collateral Damage

6:48 a.m. – Friday, 20th July 1979

The morning after the attack on the Hinckley Farm.

A few kilometres south of Kapiri Mposhi ...

Farai recoiled at the sudden burst of daylight in his face. Two dark figures loomed over him.

"*Fuma! Fuma! Kamani!* . . . Get up!" A voice rasped from above. Prodded by something hard, he writhed like a fish out of water. Not able to scream because of the tight gag over his mouth, his eyes welled with tears.

As he became accustomed to the light, he saw three men, two with rags hiding the lower half of their faces and one wearing a balaclava. Pulling him by the legs, they lifted him out of the boot and threw him into the nearby bushes like an unwanted sack of refuse. He wriggled desperately, his throat sore from his attempts to yell for help.

"Shut up! If you don't shut up right now, we'll kill you, do you understand?"

He was very afraid.

Amos inspected the area around him, he shifted a few more branches and covered the tyre tracks with some grass. Standing still, he could hear birds chirping unseen in the trees. It was a glorious morning.

Paul Mutamina and the others were with the car, well out of sight. Then Amos pulled a small cloth bag the size of his fist out of his pocket. He untied a knot and gently poured the contents into his palm. They looked like dirty fragments of broken green glass. He grinned. Things had not gone exactly to plan but he'd succeeded in his mission. Hearing shuffling sounds in the distance, he glanced over his shoulder and quickly placed the stones back into the bag and into his pocket.

❊

After Amos had made his way back to the car, he found his men standing over their captive. Paul raised his eyebrows. "What do we do with him, Boss?" Looking down at the trussed body, Amos heard a muffled groan.

"*Iwe* shut up!" Musa poked the victim hard with his shoe.

Amos got down on his haunches and gripped Farai's chin. His eyes watered and he wanted to sneeze. Then Amos slowly undid the gag over Farai's mouth, taking care not to tear the skin on his lips.

"What's your name?" he demanded.

Farai swallowed.

Amos hit him gently on the cheek with two fingers.

"What's your name?"

"Fa … Fa … Farai"

"Ah, so you're a foreigner? … One of … '*Our brothers in the struggle*'…all the way from Rhodesia, eh?" Amos removed the balaclava that had covered the lower part of his face, Farai averted his eyes. Paul, Musa and Mambwe shifted nervously behind him. Then Amos gave a wry smile. "Look at me Farai!" Farai turned his head slowly. "… we're all brothers here, aren't we?" Amos glanced over his shoulders at his three henchmen. "Are we not all brothers in the struggle against the white man?"

Farai's breathing hastened. "Plea – please, don't kill me, don't kill me… please … in the name of Jesus … I- I have two children … a wife …" Amos placed a finger over Farai's mouth.

"Farai – are you a military man? … Do you know the meaning

of 'collateral damage'?"

Sweat had made tracks down Farai's temples. "*Heeeyah*!" He breathed hard.

Amos spoke to his men. "Does any one of you know what 'collateral damage' is?" The three men exchanged confused looks. They were nervous, not grasping the point of Amos's theatrics, though they knew not to question him.

"Collateral damage, my friends, is something that is common in warfare. You people need to read books – eh? Educate yourselves." He turned back to Farai. And then with his fingers stroking the air, he explained. "Collateral damage is anything that gets caught up in the crossfire during a battle. The things that get destroyed in pursuit of victory – it's a necessary evil, you understand? Throughout history great men have known that in order to achieve great things, sacrifice is unavoidable. Sometimes it's the innocent who have to pay the price of victory." He stared at Farai for a moment, sizing him up. Then he spat on the ground and straightened himself, "We'll wait until nightfall and then we'll see what to do with our dear brother here!"

❄

Paul looked at the food inside the crumpled paper bag in his hands. There was not much – some pieces of bread, a few bananas and a portion of cooked ham. They also had a two-litre plastic container of water to share amongst them. It was Amos who'd made sure to bring some rations in case they would have to lay low for a few days. Paul plucked up enough courage to ask Amos a question. "…*ba* Boss, how long do you think we'll have to stay here?" Amos leant back against a rock and lighting a cigarette, he looked at Musa and Mambwe who were guarding their captive. "Not long … a few nights. Just until things blow over." Paul was worried, he trusted and revered Amos but little had prepared him for the events of the previous night. He had been ready to break into the Hinckley's farmhouse, rough them up a bit if they offered any resistance, but murder? … No, murder had not been in the plans.

"*Ba* Amos… why did we take him with us?" He asked nervously.

Amos placed a hand behind his head and stretched. Then drawing hard on his cigarette, he exhaled slowly, the smoke rising into the trees.

"Would you have had us leave a witness behind?"

"… nnno *ba* Amos …but it was dark… and he didn't see …"

"How can you say what he saw or didn't see, eh?"

Paul recoiled. "…so, what do we do with him now?" He regretted asking the question as soon as the words escaped his mouth.

"I told you before, we'll wait until it is dark, and then we'll deal with him. Is there a problem?"

Paul shook his head quickly "Nnnno *ba* Amos, there's no problem." He turned to leave but Amos called after him. "Mutamina!"

"Ye… yes boss"

"Let this be the last time you question my judgement. Do we understand each other?"

"… Yes, *ba* Amos … I understand… I understand perfectly."

Paul, Mambwe and Musa sat quietly a short distance away from Amos. They took turns keeping an eye on Farai a few feet from them. They had shared the small ration of food and given the lion's share to Amos. Farai had not eaten. Each man was lost in his thoughts, tense and fearful. Each man knew that they were now fugitives hunted for murder.

"We have to get rid of him." Mambwe whispered. His voice was fearful "Why did we even bring him with us?"

Musa wiped his brow, his hand shaking. Hitherto, he and his close friend Mambwe had been nothing but bit players. This time, they found themselves knee deep in something huge, something they hadn't signed up for. They had been recruited by Paul Mutamina barely a few days before. He had met with an acquaintance Discipline Kola from Kabwata Township – a ramshackle compound in the heart of the city. For those in the know, Discipline was the man whenever a job of a certain nature needed to be done. He was the one who could find individuals with particular talents. Car-jackers, burglars, pick pockets, thugs and two-bit conmen – he knew them all. It was a mystery as to why Discipline himself had never been caught by the police. Some said that it was because he worked both sides of the fence. No one knew, and no one dared to ask.

Paul had found Discipline at his usual market stall where he sold used automobile parts – bearings, gaskets, batteries and the like. He said he needed some men and a car for a job – two, possibly three, would suffice. Out of self-preservation, Discipline never asked for details – all he needed to know was what kind of skills and resources were needed and, of course, how much one was willing to pay. It took two weeks for Discipline to find a car that he claimed could not be traced, and to introduce Paul to Musa and Mambwe – two young small-time criminals eager to make a bit of money.

Lying on the ground, Farai's thoughts drifted to his two little girls playing a game of hop-scotch outside the house while his wife prepared some sadza on hot coals. He rued his decision to leave them in Bulawayo while he sought work in Zambia. So much time lost, time he would never get back. The twine tethering his hands dug deep into his wrists numbing his fingers. He felt light-headed and remembered that he hadn't eaten for many hours. Farai recalled a nurse at the rural clinic telling him that he had what she termed 'the sugar disease'. She'd explained that it was important for him to not go hungry for long periods of time or else he could collapse and lose consciousness. Farai shook the thought out of his mind – right now that was the least of his concerns. The sun was beginning to fall. He mumbled a prayer. The end was surely near.

12

Discipline

8:49 p.m.

Lusaka Central Police Station

Max arrived to find a handwritten note from Jennifer on his desk. The results of the licence plate search were now available in the records department and he needed to sign for them; a man named Frits had called saying that he was a friend of the Hinckleys – 'sounded upset and aggressive', she'd added. Max frowned, and made his way downstairs. He signed his name into a large log book and hastily opened the brown envelope, scanning through the neatly stapled two-page report. As expected, the vehicle had been reported stolen several months ago and the licence plate did not match the vehicle identification number on its chassis. Unsurprising. Many car-jackers switched plates to avoid detection, Max read on. In this case the number on the chassis was for a Volkswagen Kombi registered in Chelston, Lusaka – it too had been reported stolen over a month ago. Max rubbed his chin. There were several small auto mechanic workshops in Lusaka known to deal in stolen vehicles – spray painting, swapping plates and so on. He needed to find out if anyone had worked on this particular vehicle and he knew exactly whom to ask for this kind of information.

Discipline Kola ushered the two detectives into his living room. He immediately sent his wife and three small children to their bedrooms so that he could converse freely with the officers. He had a surprisingly luxurious home for one who merely sold used automobile parts in a market stall. He settled himself into his armchair, which faced a black and white television set on the far end of the room.

"*Mwiasenipo mukwai, Mwaisenipo mukwai.*" His eyes nervously searching their faces. Discipline always repeated everything he said. Max considered him a shifty character, the kind who would sell his firstborn child if the price was right. Nonetheless, over the years, Discipline had proved an invaluable informant, his tips had helped the police solve several intractable cases. In exchange, the police force looked the other way when it came to Discipline's own misdeeds.

Max and Ronald sat at opposite ends of a *faux*-leather sofa. "So, what brings you here officers? What brings you here officers?" Discipline asked with a sycophantic smirk, drawing his hands together as if in prayer.

Max cleared his throat. He hated being indebted to such a miscreant but at this moment he needed all the help he could get. He glanced in the direction of the corridor. Discipline's wife and children were nowhere to be seen. "We're trying to track down a suspect in a murder case." Disciplines' eyes shifted from side to side. "The crime occurred on the outskirts of the city, in Makeni, during the early hours of Friday morning … an elderly white couple were brutally killed." Max searched Discipline's face for a reaction. There was none. "We've found the vehicle which the killers used to escape the crime scene… No surprise, it's a stolen vehicle … a white Peugeot 504 station wagon. It's been worked on… the licence plate changed and it was spray painted sometime in the last month or so. So…" Max paused for emphasis, "is there anything you can tell us? Do you any have information that might help us?"

Discipline sat quietly tapping his fingers against the armrests of his chair. Then he shook his head. "No *sah*, no *sah* … I've not heard anything; not heard anything."

Max could feel Ronald's impatience growing. "Think hard. Nobody, nobody that you've seen or heard has mentioned a job of this nature in the past month or so?" Again, Discipline shook his head. "Plenty work, plenty work, *sah*. Cars come and go, come and go. Plenty accidents, plenty accidents. But no, *sah*, me no remember, no remember no white Peugeot."

Max leaned forward, "How many children do you have, Discipline?"

"…Thr… three, I have three, *sah*."

"And this beautiful house … how long have you been living here?"

"… We … we just moved in, we just moved in, *sah*."

Max did not believe that the police should threaten people but under the circumstances it was warranted. "Discipline, do you understand that if we find out that you're deliberately withholding information that would help us to solve a criminal case, you *will* be held liable for obstruction of justice and you *will* go to prison for a very long time, eh? … I'm sure you wouldn't want those children to be evicted from this …" He circled his finger in the air. Discipline scratched the back of his neck. "Now, I'll ask you one more time … and this time I want you to think very hard …"

As Max and Ronald entered their vehicle they had concluded two things: the first was that, if Discipline Kola was to be believed, then Paul Mutamina was indeed involved in the attack at Hinckley Farm for they could link him to the abandoned vehicle. The second was that Paul had at least two accomplices by the names of Musa and Mambwe and if they located Mutamina then they would surely find the others. Hence, it was imperative that they visit Chimutengo Prison where Paul had spent the last several years. This was a job for tomorrow morning but for now they would head back to HQ and see what else they could find out about Mr and Mrs Hinckley by going through the two boxes of documents obtained from their study. One thing Max still could not understand was why the robbers had resorted to so much gratuitous violence, it just didn't make sense.

9:56 p.m.

Mukushi Farm District

Frits Hubercht opened the back door to his kitchen and stepped onto his porch. He stared into the night, his last bottle of whisky in one hand. He had not stopped thinking about the murders. What had happened? What had gone wrong? Standing in the cool breeze, he fought back tears.

He thought about the telegram he had received that afternoon. Soon he'd be losing it all – the car, the house, the farm. He owed people, he owed the bank and he had lost all hope of paying them back. He brushed the thought out of his mind. What did it matter now? He had lost his two closest friends and there was nothing he could do to bring them back. He took a long hard swig from his bottle. The potent liquid burned down his throat. He brushed the wetness from his lips with the outside of his forearm. He needed to pack a few things for his journey in the morning.

13

Hail Mary

"*Fock! Fock! Fock!*" Mambwe yelled into the trees, his chest heaving. It was not yet dark, the gentle glow of dusk could still be seen through the leaves. Shaken out of their slumber, Paul and Musa staggered to their feet.

"Where is he? … Where is he? … He's gone! … He's gone! …"

"Wha … What?" Musa exclaimed.

"The guy … Farai … he's gone … he's run away!"

"What do mean?" Paul asked.

"He's gone … disappeared!" Mambwe shouted.

"But you were supposed to be watching him!" Paul shouted with anger as they all began to search the area. "It's not possible!" They rummaged through the nearby bushes like wild dogs in search of a hare but found nothing. There was no trace of him. Aghast, Paul cupped his hands behind the back of his head. "You were supposed to be watching him!" Angry and afraid, he charged at Mambwe throwing a fist at him. It landed squarely on the side of his jaw. Mambwe tumbled into the bushes. Musa grabbed Paul from behind to restrain him. Mambwe picked himself up and balled his fists ready to defend himself but Musa stopped him. "Wait! Where's *ba* Amos?"

The three men stood silently for a moment, their breathing punctuated by the sound of the wilderness around them – crickets, chirping birds and rustling leaves. They looked at where Amos had been resting only hours before but there was only the brown paper bag of food which they had left for him.

✳

Moments earlier ...

As Farai lay awake with his head on the ground. Hearing a slight movement, he opened his eyes and watched Amos as he slowly rose to his feet and scanned the area. Satisfied that his men were deeply asleep, he took a few quiet measured steps away from them and paused. Farai lay still, unsure of what to make of it all. He quickly closed his eyes. What was Amos up to and where was he going? The man retreated into the bushes and within seconds he was out of sight.

Farai felt a surge of anxiety. What was happening? Was the man going to return with a weapon to finish him off? He recalled what he had said before about *'Collateral Damage'*. Driven by fear, Farai rubbed his wrists together behind his back. The twine bore into his skin. The three men in front of him appeared to be fast asleep. Could this be his last chance? He rubbed his wrists together even harder, more frantically, ignoring the pain. His heart was beating loudly in his ears. He began to recite a prayer inside his head, '*Hail Mary, full of grace, the Lord is with thee ...*'

14

Honour amongst Thieves

Paul's head spun in relentless circles. He found it hard to believe that Amos Mushili had abandoned them. It was the ultimate betrayal, something he had not seen coming. He placed his hands over his head and winced. Disparate thoughts swirled in his mind. How could it be? Why? Had he taken the hostage with him and if so why? Had Amos turned on them? Was he on his way to report them to the authorities?

"You must know where he is!" Paul was brought back into the present by Mambwe. He could not quite see Mambwe's face in the shadows but the venom in his voice was unmistakable.

"What are you saying?"

"The two of you are in it together ... all of this is a plot to swindle us of our share of the money!" Mambwe was furious and scared in equal measure, "What did you put in that water and the food we ate? You must have drugged us! How is it that we passed out just like that? ... you and him must have planned this... this whole thing all along!"

Mambwe grabbed Paul by the shoulder but he beat it back. Paul protested. "That's ... that's madness!"

"Is it?" Musa demanded. He stepped closer to Paul. "Then how do you explain this, eh? How's it that we all slept so deeply that we didn't hear either of them leave? It doesn't add up." The tension in the air was palpable. Musa continued. "We hardly know Amos but you and him go way back ... For all we know the two of you were planning on running off with our share all along!"

"Stop talking nonsense!" Paul raised his hands. "Am I not here? Was I not sitting right next to you? ... If I had wanted to run off with your share, don't you think I'd have done so while you were sleeping?"

An uneasy silence fell in the dark space between them – crickets chirped in the grass and leaves rustled in a gentle breeze. Mambwe and Musa, weighed their options – Amos and the hostage, Farai, were missing. Had their location been compromised? Were Amos and Paul in it together? Was this all a ploy to swindle them of their share of the spoils? Was Paul telling the truth or were they being set up to take the blame for the murders?

"Shit!" Mambwe shouted. "That bastard ... you wait until I get my hands on him... I swear I'll slit his throat!"

"We have to get out of here. For all we know the police are already on their way!" Musa's voice was unexpectedly shrill.

Mambwe breathed heavily. "But where can we go?"

"I say we head back the same way we came." Musa said.

"But it took us over an hour from the main road ... we'll need to take the car."

Paul was smarting over the fact that the man he revered had left him in the lurch. "But we can't go back onto the main road, it's too risky... there'll be police everywhere by now!" He rubbed the back of his neck. "I think the best thing we can do is to head deeper into the bush on foot... our chances of slipping past the police are better that way.... Maybe even split up…"

Mambwe replied tersely. "No way! There's no way you're splitting from us. I need to keep my eye on you! We're all getting into the car"

Paul attempted to argue but Musa concurred with Mambwe and so against his better judgement he acquiesced.

Musa turned to Mambwe. "Do you know how much fuel we have?"

"I think we've enough to take us into Kapiri... once we get there we'll figure something out."

✳

81

They worked with furious haste to remove the branches they'd placed on top of the vehicle. They had no time to waste. Musa worked the naked wires below the steering wheel until the vehicle sparked into life, never had his skills as a car-jacker proved more useful. He held the steering wheel tightly, Paul sat in the seat next to him while Mambwe loomed in the back seat watching Paul's every move. He didn't trust him at all.

In the silence, the engine appeared to screech and judder as they wove their way through the dense bush. There was a quiet tension in the air, each man plotting his next move and fearful of the distinct possibility of being caught.

Eventually, they reached a level stretch of gravel. Musa pushed his foot on the accelerator and they raced down the narrow road, overhanging branches slapping against the windows. It took them close to twenty minutes to reach the tarred road leading into Kapiri.

Musa wiped his brow, his grip tightened against the steering wheel as they raced through the night. All they needed to do was to get close enough to the town, dump the car and then proceed on foot. But then suddenly, "Shit!" A police checkpoint!

❊

A female officer flagged the vehicle down. Musa lowered his window.

"Papers." She demanded sternly. She was holding a torch while her other hand was resting on the rifle slung over her shoulder. Musa reached across to the glove compartment. Paul felt the hastening of Mambwe's breathing behind him.

Musa rummaged through some papers for a few seconds before straightening up. The officer shone a light on the wad of papers in Musa's hand.

"I need your licence and registration!" She rasped, before angling the torch in Musa's face. Trembling, some of the papers dropped into his lap. As he attempted to gather them, a door in the back opened suddenly.

"*Uko! Uko!*" The officer yelled. Mambwe had made a run for it!

"*Uyo apo!*" A voice from the darkness screamed. There was a sound of rushing footsteps. "Stop! … Stop! … Hands up! … Hands up!"

A shot was fired. It crackled in the night like a firecracker. More footsteps. "Hands up!" Then a crescendo of firecrackers.

Paul and Musa were dragged out of the vehicle by several armed men hurling obscenities. They were thrust on to the ground, their faces pushed into the dirt.

DAY 3

Sunday, July 22nd 1979

15

Things Left Unsaid

2:25 a.m.

Chilenge, Lusaka

Max jumped into the river, the waves were white and frothy. Underestimating the ferocity of the currents, he was soon flung against the rocks and swept away. He struggled, trying to gain some momentum with his arms and legs, as his mouth and nose filled again and again with water. Exhausted, he began to sink. Semi-conscious, he observed a light beyond the surface of the water, obscured suddenly by the shadow of two figures. Then, he felt a hand grab him by the wrist and begin to pull him upwards to safety.

Max sat up in bed with a sudden wrenching movement, he was drenched in sweat. Mavis was sitting beside him. She gently placed her palm on his chest – it felt cool and soothing.

"It was a dream, only a dream," she said softly, offering him a glass of water. "You were having a nightmare." Max reached for the glass and drank before giving it back to her. His breathing began to slow to an even pace.

He looked at his wife gratefully, as the dream slowly began to fade.

"What time is it?" he asked.

"It's two thirty in the morning," she replied. "You were very restless, so I went to the kitchen for some water." The security lamp shining through the thin curtains gave the room a sort light. She sat quietly for a moment regarding him. "What was it? What were you dreaming about?" This was the most intimate they had been in several months. Her voice was gentle and filled with concern.

Max wiped his brow. "… It's … it's nothing really … I'll be fine … It's just that I've been really stressed at work. We have a … case …" He fabricated, sure that the Hinckley case was not the cause of his nightmares. No, it was one that had plagued him since he was twelve years old. A nightmare born of a secret. Something, only he knew about and had never revealed to anyone. Sometimes the nightmares would disappear for months, but they would always return. When times were happy, as they had been when he married Mavis, and had their first two children, they seemed to disappear altogether. But when Lindiwe died and Mavis began to drift away from him, the nightmares returned to haunt him.

Mavis was silent, watching him. There was so much unsaid between them. Max reached for her hand but she drew back. What Max didn't realise was that it was his own inability to open himself up to her – warts and all – that had formed the mortar cementing the separation between them.

16

Rumblings at the Top

7:02 a.m.

British Foreign Office, King Charles Street, Westminster, London

Secretary Owen read the security briefing in silence while his aide looked on. At thirty-eight, David Owen was the youngest cabinet minister in the British Government – a rising star in the Labour Party. As Foreign Secretary, all matters concerning the British government abroad fell under his purview. He carefully laid the sheet of paper on top of his neatly arranged desk and looked up at the young man. "Not good, not good at all." He said pointing down at the sheet of paper. "Do you understand that I'll be briefing the Prime Minister in two hours and he'll want to know about preparations for Her Majesty's trip to Africa?" The young man fidgeted nervously.

The Foreign Secretary drew a deep breath. "You do understand that her Majesty is due to travel in three days' time and this sort of thing screams of instability within the region? If we can't inspire confidence then the whole trip will have to be cancelled. Do you know what calling off such a high profile trip will do to my … and your career?"

The young administrator pulled at his collar, his neck tie suddenly feeling tight around his neck. He cleared his throat. "Sir … do you want me to summon the Zambian High Commissioner here in Kensington?"

"And what good will that do?" Secretary Owen snapped. "He won't know any bloody more than we do ... I suspect we'll have better information and more influence than he will. No, I need you to call our mission in Zambia directly. We need to get a hold of somebody high up in the Zambian government to sort this out ... we need them to put every resource they have into catching these bloody murderous thugs and put a stop to these headlines. I want you to go as high as Kaunda himself if you must! ... I can just see the papers now ... *'Zambian thieves kill former British minister's family while Her Majesty drinks tea with the President!'*"

"... Yes sir ... Right away ... I'll make some calls immediately."

Exasperated, Secretary Owen leant back in his chair. "They wanted independence and we gave it to them. Now they've got to act like a responsible government and sort this bloody mess out!"

Woodlands, Lusaka

Peter James placed the receiver back on its cradle and sank his tall lanky frame into his chair. It was not often that he received a call directly from the London office. It was not good, not good at all. He looked up at the bust of a water buffalo staring at him from the wall, a reminder of the luxurious life he had managed to carve out for himself in Africa – maids, gardeners and high tea – worlds apart from the terraced house of his youth in Derbyshire. He had been a loyal servant of the British government, serving as a diplomat but also providing valuable intelligence when needed; a man who could be trusted to hold his nerve in amoral situations. Peter sighed, he had hoped that his meeting with Chief Mbewe might hasten the local police's efforts to bring the Hinckley case to a close before news of it exploded into the British press, but he was wrong. Now he realised that more pressure needed to be exerted, he had to take the matter all the way up to State House. There was no time to waste, the issue had to be dealt with immediately, Her Majesty's trip was at stake and so was his job!

✳

Chief Mbewe hadn't finished towelling himself dry, when his wife hurriedly entered the bathroom telling him he had an urgent call. Seated on the bed, the receiver pinned to his ear, beads of water gleamed across his hairy chest and rolling belly.

"Mbewe, this is General Kalaluka."

"Ye… Yes, sir"

"Mbewe, this matter with the white couple … eh … the Hinckleys. Where have you got to? Have you apprehended the criminals responsible?"

Chief Mbewe cleared his throat. "Sir … we are currently investigating … I … I've our best man on the job, sir."

There was a short pause. "Mbewe, do you understand the sensitivity surrounding this case?"

"Yes … yes sir, I understand completely, sir"

"I have just been contacted by State House! It seems this matter has reached the attention of *ba kateka* … yes, the president himself … do you understand what this means?"

Chief Mbewe wiped his face. Even though the Inspector General had spoken in an even tone, he could sense his indignation.

"Mbewe, we need to bring this matter to a quick resolution *atini*? Otherwise we will all look like fools and we cannot allow State House to be embarrassed. Am I making myself clear?"

"Yes, sir … I understand, sir."

"We need this thing put to bed immediately, we cannot allow these murders to hang over the upcoming Heads of Government Summit. Do you understand?"

"Ye … Yes sir."

Another pause followed by a deep breath. "It's good that we understand each other. I'm counting on you, Mbewe, I have great faith in you … don't let me regret having appointed you, *fya umfwika te*?"

"Yes, sir … *fya umfwika* … loud and clear, sir!"

17

Running out of Time

8:48 a.m.

Lusaka Central Police Station

Max sat in his chair with papers strewn across his desk. He had been unable to get back to sleep and at around 4 a.m., he had decided to go to his office to continue going through the piles of papers taken from the Hinckley's study. So far, he had not come up with much, most were mundane farm accounts listing daily takings from the various livestock pens. He glanced at his watch, it was almost nine, Ronald would be arriving soon and they would be making the two and half hour drive to Chimutengo Prison. Jennifer Yumbe had made arrangements for them to meet with the Warden, one Boniface Bwembya, which had been arranged for one o'clock that afternoon. The Warden could not meet them any sooner for he was a deacon in his church and had service on Sunday mornings.

The telephone on his desk rang suddenly. Max stared at the phone for a moment wondering who would be calling his desk on a Sunday morning. "Hello? Detective Chanda speaking."

"Chanda?"

"Yes, speaking."

"Chanda. Chief Mbewe here."

"Oh ... yes sir." Max had not recognised the voice. He and the Chief rarely spoke on the phone.

"Have you seen the newspaper?" Max hesitated. He hadn't yet

seen the morning paper but from the tone of the chief's voice, he guessed that the news was not pleasant.

"*Ehm* .... no sir, I have not."

"*Fock* man!" The Chief swore. It was unusual for him to swear as he considered it to be uncouth. "The press have latched onto the Hinckley connection to the former British Home Secretary, Rab Butler. They did some digging and they know Henry Hinckley was his nephew. This is bad ... very bad. They're saying it'll be a diplomatic fiasco if the Queen visits Zambia with these killers still roaming the country ... people are calling for the whole trip to be called off!" He breathed heavily. "And now I have the Inspector General calling me at home asking what the hell is going on! ... Chanda, how close are you to rounding up these murderers? ... It's been over two days already!"

Max pulled the phone away from his ear. He weighed his words carefully. "Sir, we've made progress ... we've narrowed down our suspects but we still have some work to do ..."

"Progress? Progress? ... Damn it man! I don't want to hear about progress ... eh? I want you to bloody catch these men and put an end to this ... this ... this mess!"

The extent of the chief's exasperation caught Max by surprise. He of all people knew what went into a thorough police investigation – it took time to investigate every lead and to leave no stone unturned. "Yes sir, I'm working on it, sir ... we've identified a person of interest and I'm confident that we'll get to the bottom of it ... we ... we just need a little more time."

There was a long pause. Chief Mbewe seemed to calm himself a little. "Chanda ... I placed great faith in you ... you're my best detective. See that you don't disappoint me, Chanda. I'll keep the hounds at bay but there's only so much I can do." Max listened as Chief Mbewe took another deep breath. "Chanda, I hope to God that my faith has not been misplaced." With that he hung up.

Max carefully placed the receiver back onto its cradle. Leaning back in his chair, he felt like the world around him was collapsing and he was powerless to stop it. He glanced at his watch again –

where was Ronald? He picked up another folder from the pile on his desk and opened it. There was a black and white photograph frayed and yellowing around the edges. It was a picture of a young Henry and Laura Hinckley. He recognised them from the framed wedding picture in the living room of their farmhouse. They looked about the same age as they were then. They were standing next to each other, smiling. He turned the photograph over. In the top right hand corner he could still make out some writing in fading ink: '*Wythenshaw, 1958*'.

18

Peas in a Pod

Twenty-one years earlier...

Saturday, March 15ᵗʰ 1958

Wythenshaw, Manchester, England

Laura Ashburn peered through the window of the double decker bus, as rain glistened in the city lights. She sighed, wondering if it was a mistake to join her roommate, Mary, on what was effectively a blind date. Mary had been going to the pictures with her boyfriend Oliver, and they were to be accompanied by his friend Henry who had recently returned from abroad. The girls were both in their final year of a secretarial course at Stockport College just outside Manchester. Not one for socialising, Laura had for the most part kept to herself. That she was not shy to speak her mind did also not endear her to many of the young men in college who seemed to value congeniality above debate. Mary, on the other hand, had quickly identified Oliver as a future husband. Whether he knew it or not, she had determined that he would fit perfectly into her carefully laid plans for life in a pretty cottage in rural Merseyside. Mary had now taken it upon herself to find a match for her opinionated roommate.

The double decker bus turned on to Oxford Road and drew to a halt at the first stop. "This is where we get off." Mary said quickly and pulling up the hoods to their raincoats, they soon stepped into the drizzle. Mary led the way as they crossed the busy street and into a cobbled alley. Moments later they reached an entrance underneath a sign that read, 'The Crown Pub'.

The dimly lit space smelled of cigarette smoke, ale and damp wood. People sat in clusters around dark wooden furniture. Mary turned to Laura with a smile. "It's a grand place, I'm sure you'll like it." Laura's shoulders stiffened, she would much rather have been tucked in her warm bed with a good novel. Mary sensed her friend's unease. "Come on Laura, it'll be fine. It's just a few drinks that's all – you're not getting married to the bloke for heaven's sake!" Laura gave her a dirty look. Mary narrowed her eyes to the back of the smoke-filled room. "Olie and Henry should be here already… ah, there they are!"

Oliver was wearing a hideous red and green jumper which looked like something his grandmother had knitted for him as a Christmas gift. Giving Mary a hug and a peck on the cheek, he dutifully took her raincoat and folded it over his arm. Then Laura received a perfunctory hug before he turned to introduce his friend who stood patiently behind him. "Laura … I'd like you to meet Henry … Henry Hinckley… he's a dear old friend of mine… Henry, please meet Laura Ashburn."

Henry extended his hand. "Pleasure to meet you, Laura." She nodded and shook it, feeling his firm grip. He was not what Laura had expected. She had assumed that any friend of Oliver's would be like him – neat, kind, maybe a little stuffy, but Henry had a rugged self-assured air – she couldn't decide whether that was a good or a bad thing. As they sat down around a table, Laura noticed Henry's unbuttoned collar and rough stubble on his chin.

Oliver ordered some drinks: A pint of ale for himself, a Jonny Walker for Henry and a sherry each for the girls. After a few minutes of benign chit chat, Mary straightened her back and smiled. "So, Henry, we're all dying to hear about your adventures abroad … So exciting! Where exactly were you and what were you doing?" She gave a mischievous smile. Laura cringed.

Henry cupped his hands over his mouth as he lit a cigarette and slowly blew a smoke ring, before he answered. "I was in Northern Rhodesia. Spent six months there …"

Mary slapped Laura coquettishly on the arm. "Did you hear that? He was in the African jungle for six whole months … Oh my, weren't you afraid? … All those wild creatures … lions and tigers … I'd be so terrified!" Laura felt herself withdrawing into her body.

Henry continued, "I was working for a prospecting company. I loved it. The fresh air, the golden sunsets and breathtaking landscapes … it's unlike anything you'd see here in England … unlike anywhere else in the world, really." There was a wistfulness in his tone but Laura bridled at the romanticism with which he described colonial Africa. She pursed her lips.

"But don't you think that you were exploiting those poor Africans?" she burst out. " … I've read about how the colonies have been plundered for years by European companies pillaging their mineral resources and leaving nothing for the natives. How can you possibly justify that? Instead of standing up and trying to save them from the tyranny of colonialism you went out to participate in it!"

"Laura!" Mary exclaimed in a hushed voice.

Henry raised his hand gently, a cigarette lodged between his fingers. He grinned. "That's quite all right …" Unfazed, he looked consideringly at Laura as if seeing her for the first time. She held his gaze. "You make a good point, but what makes you think the *poor* Africans, as you call them, need saving?"

Always quick to the fray, Laura retaliated. "I just don't think it's right for Europeans, or indeed anyone, to go to a place and tell people what to do and what to believe, while plundering their resources."

If Laura thought she would draw blood, she was wrong. Henry was invigorated by a good argument. He smiled calmly. "Again, you make a good point and I agree with you …" He paused, taking a last pull of his cigarette before crushing the stub into an ashtray. " That is … except … how can you, Laura Ashburn, have such conviction that you're right, never having stepped foot in Africa, a big continent? How can you be so sure that what you've read is true?"

Laura, momentarily wrong footed, was not ready to withdraw. "You don't know where I've been and where I haven't."

Henry sipped his whisky before putting his glass down gently on the table in front of him. "Well? ... Have you?"

Laura shifted uncomfortably in her seat as Mary and Oliver stared at her waiting for her response.

"Have I what?"

"Been to Africa?"

"… My point is that we need to let the Africans live their own lives and make their own choices. This whole business of colonialism has only brought misery and oppression … how can we be trusted to make decisions affecting others when we can't get things right here in Britain – look at what's going on with all the bickering between Labour and the Tories?" Henry gave a wry smile. He knew that this was the closest he would get to an admission of defeat from this sparky red head.

Mary interrupted the banter. "Oh, honestly you two, can we please stop with all the political talk and drink up? ... Olie, isn't it time we left for the pictures? ... I for one can't wait to see that handsome Tony Curtis …" She turned and smiled playfully at Oliver. "…oh but he's not as handsome as you my dear."

19

Laura, Henry and Frits

9:12 a.m.

Great North Road, five miles north of Lusaka

Frits had left his farm at the crack of dawn and was now entering the outskirts of Lusaka heading south on the Great North Road. Throughout the long hours of the solitary drive, he kept thinking about Laura and Henry, images of their bludgeoned bodies flashing through his mind. How had things gone so desperately wrong?

Suddenly, a stray dog darted into view across the road. He swerved hard but not before hearing a thud. Steadying the car, he stopped several feet ahead. He peered through the rear-view mirror but couldn't see the animal. It must have disappeared into the bushes. He slowly stepped out of the car and inspected the front of the vehicle. There was a dent on the right fender but nothing else. Slowly, Frits walked along the side of the road back to the spot where he'd hit the dog, his heart beating furiously as he searched the bushes. Nothing. Finally, he walked heavily back to his car and slumped into the driver's seat. Leaning his forehead against the steering wheel, he sighed. Things were falling apart and it was taking everything within him to hold it together.

Three months earlier...

April 1979

Hinckley Farm, Makeni

Frits could see Laura from the driveway standing outside the front door to their farmhouse as he approached. She was smiling broadly and waved at him. He parked his Land Rover a short distance from the house. The last time he had visited, Henry had just suffered a severe stroke. Laura's subsequent letters had indicated that he was doing better but was confined to a wheelchair and had some difficulty speaking.

"My dear Fritsy, it's so lovely to see you again!" Laura said raising her arms.

"It must be something in your water, hey, because you look prettier every time I see you, Laura." Frits flattered her for, in truth, Laura had aged since their last encounter. It was clear that her husband's illness had taken its toll.

"Oh, enough of that." She said waving a quick hand in front of her face. "Flattery will get you everywhere!" Frits encircled her small frame in his embrace. "It feels like ages since I last saw you." She took a step back and tapped him gently on his stomach, "… and I see you're still eating that pap." He chuckled.

"Yah, well it's not going to get any smaller with me staying here for a week, hey!" He regarded her for a moment. Her eyes had lost their lustre. "How is he?"

Laura forced a smile. "We're managing." She said, her eyes skipping his gaze. "He's resting … but he'll soon be up to take his medicine."

They entered the house through a wooden door that was propped open by a folded newspaper. The parquet tiles on the floor were polished as always all the way from the small landing into the living room. "Nawakwi has your room prepared." Laura said as she called to the maid to fetch his bag from the car. "When she comes back, I'll ask her to bring us a hot pot of tea and we can sit out in the garden, if that's okay with you?"

"Sounds perfect. Let me just take a leak and I'll join you outside, hey."

✳

They sat underneath an avocado tree a few yards from the back of the house cooled by a soft breeze. Nawakwi had laid a silver tray and the tea was just as Laura had taught her to make it, hot and strong. A white kitchen towel covered a plate of small ham sandwiches sliced into perfect triangles – again just the way the madam liked them.

Laura sipped her tea peering across at the open field. A line of farmworkers could be seen in the distance bent over knee-high crops. Several feet to her left was the kennel where her two boerboels, Chanter and Whiskey, slept at night. She spoke wistfully into the air. "It always seems bizarre to me that people will travel half way around the world to find a home; and one where they own more land and property than the people whose ancestors this land belongs to? I love it, but it also makes me very uncomfortable."

Frits shifted in his seat. "Yah, Laura, but I'm not sure you're right, hey. My ancestors have been on this continent as long, sometimes longer than the blacks … I have as much right to this land as anyone, isn't it." He leaned forward and took a sandwich from beneath the kitchen towel.

Laura kept her gaze trained to the distance. "I mean doesn't it bother you sometimes that here we are, white in a black man's land, living better than the black man himself?"

Frits swallowed the sandwich in two bites before washing it down with his tea. "Yah, Laura, what's gotten into you, hey? You know it's not that simple, I mean just look around you … lots of rich blacks now… they've taken over everything, hey. Nowadays if you're white and trying to do business… you can forget it … you're screwed! They say Independence… well let me tell you, it's independence for the black politicians, that's what it is; not for anyone else. If you don't believe me … you go to some of these *bledy* minister's houses and you'll see just what I mean."

"But Fritsy … I just think when Henry and I stayed behind in '64 we hoped to see a country that was more equal. A place where

blacks, whites, Indians and whoever else could prosper together…
that was why I protested with the women at the airport. But now
it feels like whites still get preferential treatment over most blacks
with only the few at the top enjoying all the fruits of the hard-fought
independence."

"So, what are you saying, Laura? You want to give up your farm?
Or maybe you *wanna* give up the maid and the servants too?" They
both instinctively glanced back at the house. Nawakwi was cleaning
dishes in the kitchen sink out of earshot.

Laura sighed. "I don't know what I'm saying, Fritsy. Lately …
ever since …" She turned briefly to look at Frits and then stared back
at the field. "I've just been thinking a lot lately. Thinking about the
choices we've made, the things we've done …" She paused and stared
into the distance.

Frits frowned. "Laura, are you all right, hey? … You're not making
much sense … is there something you *wanna* tell me?" Laura shook
her head. A motion which seemed to pull her out of her reverie.

"It's nothing …" She glanced at her wrist. "… oh, is that the
time? … I'd better go check on Henry, it's almost time for his
medicine."

✳

9:55 a.m.

Central Police Station, Lusaka

Max hung up the telephone and leant back in his chair. It was as
he'd expected. The Lundazi District police confirmed that neither
Paul Mutamina nor his family had been seen in their village for
over a year. Clearly the story about Mutamina's wife and family
having gone to their village was not true. Had Mutamina ginned
up a plan to whisk his family into hiding ahead of the attack on
Hinckley Farm? This news, coupled with the fact that the police
affidavit describing Paul Mutamina's previous arrest for attempted
larceny a few years ago was scant on details, made it even more
important to visit Chimutengo Prison. Max hoped that speaking
to the warden, prison guards and fellow inmates might yield some

nuggets of information that could help them locate Mutamina.

The door to the office opened suddenly and Ronald hurried into the office without knocking and out of breath. Maxwell glanced at his watch. Ronald sounded unusually apologetic. "Morning boss … sorry I'm late… the minibus got stuck … there are roadworks everywhere; they're cleaning up for the Queen and the upcoming summit."

Max raised his hand. He knew what a commotion the impending summit and the Queen's visit was causing. Everything was being cleaned up and straightened out. "No need for apologies … you're here now … we need to head out to Chimutengo Prison right away … I'll brief you about developments as we go."

"Yes… yes, of course, boss."

Max rose and as he did so, he recalled the note from Jennifer concerning a gentleman who was coming to see him that morning. He paused before deciding that he would leave a message for him at the front desk.

10:12 a.m.

The junior officer at the front desk held his pen suspended above a page in an open appointment book. "… *ehn* … your name again *sah*?"

"Hubercht – H-U-B-E-R-C-H-T … Frits Hubercht."

The officer was a little intimidated by the burly white man standing above him. He printed the name carefully into the notebook before finally looking up. "Can I call another detective to speak with you, *sah*?"

Frits shook his head emphatically. "No … no, I need to speak to the detective in charge. What time will he be back?"

"I'm not sure *sah* … you just missed him … he just left for an appointment out of town … but said you can either call him or see another officer in …" Frits shook his head again. The officer adjusted his hat. "… maybe he'll be back in the evening … but it is Sunday *bwana* so I'm not *shuwa*."

20

Chimutengo

1:14 p.m.

Chimutengo Prison, Lusaka Province

Detective Max Chanda and Ronald sat across from Warden Boniface Bwembya – his office exuded piety. His desk was clear, save for an open diary and a clunky rotary telephone to his left. He had two silver pens neatly placed in the top left pocket of his coat. There was a plaque above his head on the wall behind him, which read, 'JESUS LIVES', in bold typeface. Warden Bwembya had a round face, the skin on his cheeks puckered with tiny pock marks which made him look older than he was. He straightened the lapels on his jacket before stroking the air with his hands. "So how may I assist you gentlemen on this glorious day which the Lord has given us?"

Max leaned forward. "Thank you for meeting us at such short notice and for making time on a Sunday." The warden nodded. "We're investigating a very urgent case …"

Warden Bwembya nodded again. "Indeed, my secretary informed me that the matter was very urgent … I'm at your disposal gentlemen. What can I do to assist you?"

Max patted his chest. "Thank you … we have cause to believe that one of your former inmates may have been involved in a fatal attack two nights ago."

Warden Bwembya sighed deeply. "I wish I could say that I'm surprised gentlemen, but unfortunately, these are the men who find themselves at Chimutengo. Although we do our best to reform our inmates, many of them have hearts that have been blackened by the fires of hell … I'm afraid to say that many are lost, taken by the evil one." He grabbed the air in front of him in a tight fist. "If only these young men would repent and believe in the one true saviour …" He raised his index finger and strummed the space above his nose. "… the one true Messiah, Jesus Christ!"

Ronald who had hitherto not said a word, mumbled an "Amen."

Max continued. "The inmate's name is Paul Mutamina."

Ronald chimed in "He was in Chimutengo from April nineteen seventy-five to …" He flicked through a ring-bound notepad. "… to October seventy-seven."

The Warden frowned. "That name does not ring any bells with me, but you must understand, we have many prisoners who come and go." He pushed his seat back and rose from his seat exposing his belly. "Let me check … we keep detailed records on each of our inmates … we've done so since before Independence." He said it proudly as if it was something extraordinary; prisons were supposed to keep records, thought Max.

Warden Bwembya left the room for about ten minutes, but it felt longer. When he returned, he was holding a thin manila folder. He sat back in his chair and opened it. "*Ehm* let's see … Paul Mutamina … was convicted for attempted robbery … arrived 25 April, 1975 … released October 1977." He flicked through some loose sheets of paper, licking his thumb after each page. "This is a medical report … 2 January '76 … suffered malaria … admitted for two nights in the infirmary." He thumbed through yet more pages before picking up a sheet and flicking it repeatedly from side to side. "This one is a release form listing personal effects … shirt, trousers, belt, wrist watch … nothing much." He looked up at the two detectives. "Is there anything in particular you would like to find out?" He began to straighten the sheets of paper and place them back into the folder. He handed it over to Detective Maxwell who in turn gave it to Ronald, who immediately began to burrow through it.

Max scratched his chin before straightening himself in his chair.

"Warden, we were also hoping to speak to some of your guards and perhaps a few of the inmates who might have interacted with Mutamina. You see, we're trying to gather as much information as possible about him. In my experience, it's usually the smallest of details that lead to a case being solved or a suspect apprehended."

The warden nodded his head. "Yes, yes of course. You have our full co-operation, I can take you out to see our head prison guard and he will ensure that you speak with whomever you choose." Max thanked the man and they all promptly rose from their seats. Just then, the telephone rang – a chorus of over eager bells that interrupted the conversation. Warden Bwembya excused himself before answering it.

"Good afternoon, Warden Boniface Bwembya speaking …" He listened for a few seconds and then stretched his hand out to pass the receiver to Max. "Detective Chanda … it's for you."

Surprised, Max circled his fingers over the moulded plastic and pinned it against his ear. "Hello, this is Detective Chanda …" He listened intently for several seconds before finally nodding his head. "I see … I'll start off right away." Max handed the receiver back to the warden. "They've found him."

Ronald looked up, "Found who?"

"Mutamina … He's at Kapiri Central Police Station right now. He was apprehended at a police checkpoint with two others … apparently one of them was shot while trying to escape."

Warden Bwembya placed the receiver onto its cradle. "So, then, is your investigation over?"

Max shook his head slowly. "Apparently, there's a fourth suspect who's still on the run … they say he's quite possibly the ring leader … his name is Mushili …"

"Hey - yah!" Warden Bwembya exclaimed. "Did … did you say Mushili … Amos Mushili?"

The two detectives glanced at each other.

"You know him?" Ronald asked.

The warden raised his hands. "Amos Mushili was a prisoner right here in Chimutengo … everybody knows him … that man is a devil … a real troublemaker!"

21

In the Bush

Nitipwa Rural District, a few kilometres south of Kapiri Mposhi

A yellow-billed kite circled overhead in the cloudless sky high above the trees. Three village girls with *chitenges* knotted around their waists walked along a narrow footpath which they had used countless times before. They were returning from a nearby river, each girl delicately balancing a calabash on her head, and deep in conversation when one of them stopped abruptly. She had noticed something.

"*Shhh imwe ... ichongo.*" She whispered narrowing her eyes as she examined the bushes several feet away from them. It was. It couldn't be. Surely it wasn't the body of a man in the flickering shadows.

"*Ninshi?* ... What is it?" Asked one of the girls, holding her calabash firmly with one hand and pointing into the distance with the other.

"*Apo ... pali umuntu* there's someone there ... a man ..."

All three girls focused their eyes to the same spot and sure enough they could see a man lying in the bush.

"Is he drunk?"

"Should we wake him?"

This suggestion was promptly overruled. Deciding to leave well alone, they hastened along the footpath to their village.

✳

Two young men stood at a clearing in the woods. One wore a thin unbuttoned shirt and wielded a sharp axe in his right hand. The other, a taller man, had long sinuous arms and wore a knitted skull cap.

"They said it was somewhere around here." The first man said as he examined the trees. They had been called from the nearby field where they had been chopping wood for charcoal. The three girls spotting them before they reached home had told them about the body in the woods. Intrigue and wanting to impress the girls, had prompted them to investigate, but they couldn't see anything.

"I wonder if they imagined him. Who in their right mind would be sleeping in the bush alone – that is, assuming he's not dead."

"Perhaps one who is drunk?"

He shook his head. "We're the only village within five kilometres of here, where would he've come from? Everyone we know is out working in the fields now." It was a good point, the girls' story appeared fanciful. "Let's just go back, eh? … that wood won't chop itself."

The young man with the axe cleared some low hanging branches as he took a step forward into the trees. His eyes searched the area one more time when through the crackling of his feet on the dry leaves, he heard a feeble voice.

"Help … help me … please … someone help me…"

The young man squeezed his fist over the neck of his axe and took a step towards the sound. "Over there … I can see something over there …" he called out to his friend.

The man was alive but he appeared badly in need of medical attention. "What's happened?... are you hurt?" They asked him. His forehead was sweaty, his eyes bloodshot.

Weakly, the man responded. "I … I was kidnapped by criminals …They were going to kill me … but I escaped." He said taking several deep breaths. "I … I need to get to a doctor… I'm sick…"

The two young men looked at each other. Unsure of what to do next. "Who kidnapped you?"

The man did not respond, he merely shook his head.

"Who are you? … What's your name?"

The injured man swallowed hard before mustering, "Fa … Fa

… Farai" His voice faltered. "I …I need to see … a doctor … doctor…" And then he seemed to lose consciousness.

The two woodcutters looked at each other nervously. "Let's take him with us." Fearing the worst, they propped him between them, placing his arms over their shoulders and carrying his languid frame back to their small settlement. When they arrived, they laid the man on a reed mat in the cool shade in front of one of the mud huts. The children who had been playing nearby soon gathered to observe the spectacle.

"*Ita bana* Sikazwe!" The man with the knitted cap yelled hurriedly at a small boy with tattered shorts. The boy pulled his shorts around his hip and sped towards a set of mud huts in the back. A few moments later he returned with a stout elderly woman in his wake. The gathering parted to make way for *bana* Sikazwe. As she reached the man, he retched. Tightening her *chitenge,* she knelt over the ailing man. His face and chest were wet with sweat. She examined him for a moment, she noticed hives beginning to form over his exposed forearms. She laid her palm over his forehead and opened his eyelids. Everyone remained silent in anticipation.

"How long since you find him?" she asked. The two men looked at each other.

"We find him just now, now … we bring him fast, fast but we don't know for how long he stay there."

She unbuttoned the man's shirt, placed her ear on his chest and listened for a few seconds. She could hear his heart beating. Finally, she straightened herself and looked up at the two men, "He must see the doctor." The two men exchanged glances. They knew what that meant, they would have to carry him several kilometres, then stand by the roadside and try and hitch a ride into Kapiri Mposhi and the nearest clinic. The journey would take a long time. Not many cars would stop for three men, one of whom was clearly sick.

It took them over an hour to reach the main road. Given the multiple times they had to stop to rest, it was an impressive feat. The man had remained stable, although dipping in and out of consciousness. Fortunately, they soon hailed down a grey Bedford lorry with an open back. Thanking the driver, and explaining that the man was ill, they placed him on top of some empty sacks before jumping in to sit beside him. The sick man closed his eyes, he appeared weaker with every passing minute. They were worried he would not make it. The driver set off for Kapiri, the loud engine rattling the rusted exterior of the vehicle as it blew blue fumes into the air. About twenty minutes later, they were stopped at a checkpoint. Three armed policemen circled the truck. They asked the driver and each passenger to produce their identification papers.

"And what of this one?" The officer asked with a scowl on his face. He pointed at the man lying in the back of the open truck. "What's wrong with him?"

"He is sick *sah* ... very sick *sah*, we take him to see doctor, *sah*."

The officer paused for a moment as if deciding what the appropriate response should be. "No matter ... I need to see ID now, now!"

One of the samaritans quickly dug into the man's pockets. It had not occurred to either of them to do this before and the young man hoped he might find something that would placate the overbearing officer. The first pocket was empty but the second yielded a brown wallet which he handed nervously to the policeman.

After several seconds, he produced a piece of paper which he unfolded. It was a temporary driving permit, the kind issued to foreigners before they are given a full driver's licence from the Zambian government. The name on the affidavit read: 'Farai Winston Muguru'. He looked at the sick man lying on the floor of the lorry, his forehead with an oily sheen of sweat. "He's a foreigner?" The men remained silent, unsure of what to say. Perhaps feeling pity, the officer sucked his teeth and folded the piece of paper back into the wallet, which he abruptly handed back to them. "You can go!"

✳

There were only two nurses manning the makeshift clinic across the road from the only drugstore in the vicinity. A long line of mostly women and children snaked past a rusted wire fence which had once enclosed a now defunct municipal building. The words 'CHIPATALA' were painted crookedly on one of the exterior walls. Weary looking patients sat outside waiting to be called back in to receive whatever scant medicines were available on the day. The attention of the people gathered outside the clinic was suddenly captured by three men in the distance drawing closer from the main road. Two of the men, one tall and one short, had a man propped between them. The man in the middle looked to be in desperate need of immediate medical attention. The crowd at the door parted to make way for the motley crew.

"Doctor … *ba* doctor …" one of the men said hurriedly as they entered the building. They soon made it to the front of a consultation room where a young man rose from a wooden bench to allow the sick man a seat, as he could barely stand. They waited several minutes before the door opened and a woman in a *chitenge* exited with a small child in her arms.

"Next!" Came the call from the nurse inside the room and Farai was ushered in.

22

Hearts Apart

8:02 p.m.

Chilenge, Lusaka

There was a sound of rattling keys outside the front door before it opened. Mavis Chanda looked up from the open page of the book she was reading to her son. Chipasha sat cross-legged next to his mother in the middle of the sofa. "*Tata!*" Chipasha exclaimed. Since Max had been assigned to the Hinckley case, his son had scarcely seen him as he left before dawn and returned way past his bedtime. "Eh-eh-eh … be careful, don't fall over." Mavis cautioned but the boy springing to his feet had run and jumped into his father's arms. Maxwell gave a broad smile as he lifted the little boy off his feet. Few things gave him more joy than a welcome from this little one. "Have you been a good boy to your mother?" Chipasha nodded.

"*Tata*, where have you been?" The question caused Max to look over his shoulder at his wife. Their eyes met for a moment but neither could hold their gaze.

A sense of sadness tugged at Mavis. It pained her to think that their family was slowly falling apart, fraying at the seams. Had their son noticed the growing coldness between his parents? Was he aware of his father's impulse to be away, to always find some reason to be busy, anything to be absent from home?

"*Tata*, today we went to church and we learned about how Jesus made lots of bread." Chipasha announced triumphantly. Max chuckled. "You mean how Jesus performed a miracle with loaves of bread and fish to feed the crowd of five thousand?" Chipasha nodded as he fiddled with a button on his shirt. Max placed him back on his feet and turned to his wife.

Mavis spoke first. "You're back early." He nodded. An awkward silence fell broken only by the murmur of the television. Mavis looked at Chipasha. "Go to your bedroom and change, we'll finish later."

The little boy paused for a moment. "Can't I watch T.V.?" He asked looking up at his father. "Yes, if you go and change quickly." Mavis responded. She watched as her son hurried to his room. "*Mwabombeni bashi* Chipasha ... how was work?" Mavis asked. Her eyes fixed on a point near her feet. "There's been a development in the case we're investigating." Max replied. "We believe we've had a breakthrough today ... key suspects have been apprehended near Kapiri ..."

✳

Max unzipped a small beige suitcase and placed it on the bed. Opening it, he began to place some clothes inside it. "It's an emergency..." He explained. "It's important that I go there personally."

"... but do you have to leave right away ... tonight, I mean?" There was frustration in Mavis' voice.

"There's no time to waste, every minute counts in this case. We must round up everyone involved before ..."

Mavis raised her hands to her face. "It's always an emergency whenever it's to do with your work, but when it comes to dealing with your family ... the people who matter ... you're ... you're never present!" Her sudden outburst surprised him. This was the most confrontational, she had ever been with him. Her words caught his tongue. Mavis had been brought up in the old traditions of how a *good* woman, a *good* wife, was supposed to behave. She always constrained herself, never speaking her mind, forever choosing to defer to him in all matters of consequence. She had done it so often that if her words were attached to her spine, she would have keeled over from the weight of things unsaid. 'Value harmony above all else' is what, *bana fimbusa,* the wise old women had taught her, but she had paid a price for it. When she lost her baby, the child who she had left in Max's charge, she had not expressed the full extent of her grief. In so doing, pain and anger had festered like a venom that needed to be expunged before it killed her. In all of it, Max had chosen to keep his distance, emotionally vacant, unreachable. With each passing day her resentment towards him had grown.

Max turned to her angrily, "Is that what you think of me? You think I don't care about this family? ... How can you say such a thing? ... Everything ... everything I do is for this family! Every day, I go out there ... it is for this family ... it's for you and that little boy!" He pointed to the door.

Mavis looked away. Her shoulders tense, her lips trembling. "We can't continue like this ... we just can't *bashi* Chipasha ..." Her words were soft but deliberate.

"What are you saying?"

Mavis shook her head slowly, a solitary tear racing down her left cheek. "We ... we just cannot continue this way." She stood up from the edge of the bed, the metallic springs creaking underneath her. She walked the few steps to the door and placed her hand over the knob.

Max lowered his voice. "Mavis ... listen to me ... listen ... I know things ... you ..." his words petered to a halt before he could complete his sentence. Mavis stood with her fingers circled around the door knob. For a moment she held the hope that he might open himself up to her, pave a way for them to start a dialogue that might begin to heal old wounds. She was wrong. He turned to his suit case. "I ... I need to go ... we'll talk when I return ... I promise ... we'll talk."

23

The Story of Maxwell Chanda

Twenty-five years earlier...

December, 1954

Mpika District, Northern Rhodesia

The rusted metallic bus shuddered to a halt in front of a row of market stalls along Great North Road. It was dusk and there was the usual hubbub of women in *chitenges* and *doeks* sweeping underneath wooden stands and packing away their unsold vegetables and dried fish. The busy chatter of marketeers filled the air – wives discussing their plans for what to prepare for their husbands and babies slung to their backs crying to be fed. Young Maxwell Chanda sat up in his seat next to the window and peered at the busy scene outside. He nudged his little brother on the shoulder. "Abel... Abel, *twafika*, we've arrived."

Max had just turned eleven a month earlier, Abel was seven and due to start Standard 1 the following January. This was the first time they had travelled by themselves; in fact, it was their first time to venture outside of the Copperbelt province. After the school year had ended, their mother decided that it would be good for her boys to go and stay with their grandmother, *nakulu* Chiwaya, who lived in her home village. The boys' father had protested arguing they were too young to take the two-day bus journey by themselves; and whatever would they do for three weeks in a village, since they were such urban children? Mother had gotten her way, she felt it important for her boys to discover their roots, and so here they were.

Passengers squeezed out of the bus eager to stand watch as ill-mannered call-boys pulled down contraband from the overhead carriage. Heavy laden sacks wrapped tightly with twine were lowered from the rooftop and set on the dusty ground. Max and his brother watched as opportunistic boys hustled to assist the elderly with their luggage for a fee. Upon securing their duffle bag, Max searched the crowd for their grandmother who was to meet them. It was two years since *nakulu* Chiwaya had visited them on the Copperbelt and Max hoped he would recognise her. Moments later, he saw an elderly woman with a familiar face walking towards them. She looked older and more wrinkled than he remembered – the hunch on her back more pronounced, but as she drew closer, he was certain it was she.

"*Abo baleisa*!" Max said pointing. Tired from the long journey, Abel simply yawned and rubbed his eyes Max slung his bag over his shoulder and took a few steps towards the old woman, and as he did so, she smiled, and called "*Iyee*!" her voice gravelly from chewing tobacco. Spreading her arms wide, she embraced her two grandsons. *Iyee, kuku, kuku, mwe beshikulu bandi …kuku*!" She said as she kissed them repeatedly. Max smelt a warm waft of old wood and smoke as his face was pressed against her chest.

Nakulu Chiwaya lived approximately eight kilometres north of the bus station. It was a journey they would have to make on foot, and as the sun began to set. She led the way along a narrow path through the low hanging trees and tall bushes. There were muddy puddles along the way and the smell of early rain hung in the air. Max hastened behind the old woman, while little Abel struggled to keep pace. Grandmother Chiwaya had a surprisingly sprightly gait for a woman her age – it was clear that she was accustomed to the more challenging life of the village.

Darkness fell as soon as the sun dropped behind the hills. And Max quickly realised he should follow the sound of her breathing and the rhythmic clicking of her anklets. After what seemed like an eternity, they reached a clearing where they could see two mud huts separated by a central charcoal fire which glowed luminously in the dark. *nakulu* Chiwaya announced that they had arrived. A large pot was set on top of the fire with several women and children milling around it. The smell of dried fish drifted through the air, a welcome aroma for the two boys who were now very hungry. Abel tugged hastily at his brother's shirt. *"Ba* Max, *nga inganda yili kwisa?"* He asked wanting to know where the main house was located. Max brushed off his little brother's question, admonishing him for his stupidity, although the same thought had crossed his mind. Abel's face fell. Max immediately regretted being so harsh. He put his arm around his little brother and pointed towards one of the huts, "We'll be sleeping in one of those," he said, "with our cousins. It'll be fun, you'll see."

That evening, the boys were introduced to members of their extended family – more names than they could possibly remember. When supper was served, Max and Abel were made to sit with the other children gathered in a circle on a reed mat. A steaming mound of *nshima* was placed in the centre of the circle next to a single bowl of dried fish. A prayer was said and they quickly dug into their food. It didn't take long for the two brothers to realise that they couldn't compete with the speed at which their village cousins ate. Three little girls sitting across from Max and Abel huddled together in the dim light whispering and giggling amongst themselves. It seemed that the town boys were a curiosity in the humble village setting.

To Max's consternation, mornings in the village began in darkness. The daily ritual was for the boys to be shaken out of their sleep before the crack of dawn. The first chore of the day was fetching water from the nearby river, a good thirty-minute walk, which Max, Abel and their cousins made with large plastic containers. An arduous task, it was only made palatable by the fantastical tales the children told about witches and wizards that roamed the countryside. Abel always leant more tightly into his brother's side as he listened dumbfounded and frightened of the mysterious beings lurking in the dark.

Abel looked up to his older brother. In his eyes, Max always seemed to have the best ideas and was the one all the children admired back in their township. Max could run the fastest, dribble his way through the tightest defences and score goals at will on the dusty field. The patch of ground on which they played soccer was lined on three sides by breeze-block mineworker homes. They lived on the far end of Section 6 in a unit facing the open field. A short distance behind the homes was a row of communal bathrooms which, depending on the time of day, wreaked of human ordure. These paltry living conditions were reminiscent of British colonial rule – a window into the lack of compassion with which the white master viewed the African worker.

Max's mother made sure to emphasise that he was responsible for looking after his younger brother. "He's the only brother you have … the only one… you must look after him," she would say as she scrubbed their crockery in a metallic container outside their home. "Abel looks up to you … always make sure you take care of him."

For the most part Max and Abel enjoyed their stay in the village. Life in the countryside was very different to what they were used to in the township. They had been able to forage through the woods in search of wild birds and they learned how to use rubber slingshots. They had collected *inswa* – the flying ants when the rains came and climbed trees to pick fruits like *amasafwa* and *amasuku*. Time had flown by; in only two days, they would have to return home. It was just after midday, the sun large in the clear sky. The adults were back from working in the fields, taking refuge from the heat. Recognising what little time they had left, Max wanted to go out into the forest to hunt for birds. Despite asking several times, none of the other children would go, all complaining of the heat. Not one to be deterred, Max decided to go alone. Slingshot in hand, he started in the direction of the bush. Abel chased after him along the footpath, it was an opportunity for him to impress his older brother.

As the two brothers ventured deeper into the woods, Abel began to pepper his brother with questions. "*Ba* Max … where are we going? … How far are we going? *Ba* Max, do you think we will catch a bird? … How many? *Ba* Max, do you think we can catch a very big bird? … A big bird like this?" He asked stretching his little hands as far apart as he could. The never-ending questions irritated Max. He admonished his little brother for asking too many questions but Abel would not stop.

"*Ba* Max … I can catch a big one … can you let me catch the first one?… How far are we going? …Have you walked this way before? *Ba* Max … *Ba* Max …"

They soon reached the outer banks of the river a little further downstream from where they normally drew water.

"*Ba* Max … *Ba* Max … Are we going to cross the river? Are there crocodiles in the river? *Ba* Max, do you think you can swim across?"

Annoyed, Max turned to Abel. The little boy's eyes were wide with excitement. Max replied, "What do you think, eh? … Of course I can! …I know I can swim across, but can you?" Abel nodded his head. Max laughed. "No you can't … just look at how fast that water is flowing, eh? This is not for *little* boys … it's not for a *small* boy like you!"

Abel protested. "I'm not a small boy!"

Max sucked his teeth. "Don't waste my time... we both know you can't make it across … it's not for small boys."

"I'm not a small boy and I can do it … I … I can make it." Abel's eyes were glassy with tears.

"All right, if you are so sure, then show me … show me you're not scared of swimming across, eh!" Max took several steps forward until he was standing right on the edge of the embankment. He turned. Abel was rooted to the same spot, he appeared dwarfed by the tall grass – his little chest heaving "Come on … show me, eh … show me what you can do… prove to me that you're not scared!" Abel took a tentative step forward.

"Come on! Show me you're not a small boy!"

After a couple more tentative steps, Abel stood alongside his brother at the edge of the river. They peered down at the rushing water – shimmering waves foamed over grey rocks. Driftwood raced into view and disappeared into the distance. Max turned to look at his little brother standing next to him. He felt a rising tide of regret as he remembered his mother's words: *'He is your only brother . . . he looks up to you . . . take care of him.'* Then suddenly, without warning, the ground beneath Abel's feet gave way. In an instant, he was in the water being swept away by the treacherous waves. Max jumped in after him!

The waves pushed Max back against the rocks, hitting his head. Pain coursed through his skull. He lifted his head above the waterline and caught a glimpse of Abel flapping his hands. Max fought desperately against the waves beating his arms and legs from side to side but they were too strong. He felt himself losing the battle. He gasped for air but water filled his nose and mouth. There was pressure against his chest as if a large weight had been placed on top of him. His arms grew tired. He began to sink. The sunlight up above him was retreating – all seemed lost. Then, out of nowhere, he saw two oblong faces momentarily obscuring the light. He felt a firm hand grab his wrist and then he started to draw closer to the light. That was the last thing he remembered.

Mourners gathered underneath a green tarpaulin tent outside the Chanda's home in the township. The house was too small to accommodate everyone, so many of them spilled into the muddy street. Some sat on chairs while others found loose concrete blocks which they carried from the abandoned renovation work on the communal toilets. Max's mother lay prostrate on the floor of the living room surrounded by a multitude of women in *chitenges* and *doeks*. Her eyes were swollen with tears that had not stopped falling for days. The men had made a fire outside and were discussing the burial arrangements as well as the day's politics. They talked about the Federation and how they believed it would not last. Some said it was impossible for the British to rule Northern and Southern Rhodesia as one country with Nyasaland. Others predicted the end of apartheid rule and looked forward to a time when Africans would rule themselves. "Self-rule now!" is what they said. Still others shook their heads saying the white man would never let the black man rule himself. Max sat on a patch of grass next to his father, his head sunk into his chest. Max's father appeared broken, a man unable to find an answer to the tragedy that had befallen his family.

It had been two men on their way back to work in the fields who had rescued Maxwell. They had spotted him from a distance drowning in the river and raced to his aid. They had pulled him out and laid him on the river bank. He was unconscious but still breathing. Abel had not been so fortunate. His body was discovered half a mile downstream amongst the tall reeds pinned against a fallen tree. When Max came to several hours later, he learned of his brother's demise. When asked to give an account of what had happened, he told a lie. He said that they had gone hunting for wild birds and Abel had wondered off by himself to the river bank and fallen into the water. Max described how he had tried to save his brother. However the truth of what had happened on that day would be a dark secret that would haunt Max from that day forward.

24

Square Pegs in Round Holes

6:13 p.m.

Kwacha Motel, Lusaka

The rolling black and white picture on the television screen steadied into an uneasy balance. Frits turned a broken knob left and then right again before cursing at the screen. "*Bledy* useless ... everything in this place is *kak!*" He slapped the side of the wooden box in frustration. The body of a man sitting at a news desk was momentarily split in two before merging again. He moved to an armchair in front of the television and sunk into the seat. The stained threadbare armrests spoke of past occupants who, like him, would have been unable to afford better. The hubbub in the city due to the impending Heads of Government summit meant that there were no vacancies in any of the reputable hotels and prices had gone up everywhere – still, it was unusual for a white man to stay in such an establishment. He stretched his legs on top of a wooden coffee table and stared at the screen. His thoughts drifted to the telegram he had received the previous day: '*Lawyers contacted. Expect to receive formal summons*'. It was just the latest in a string of threatening messages from his bank. Over the past year everything seemed to crumble in front of him. The life he had worked hard to build over so many years was slipping through his fingers. He had kept each telegram in a folder underneath his bed. Over several months, the telegrams had increased in frequency and sharpened in tone. At first they had been gentle reminders that he was past due on his loan payments, then later they had become pointed threats that his farm would be repossessed if he failed to pay in full.

Times had changed since Independence. The new indigenous government had little patience for white prospectors like Frits and his friend Henry Hinckley who they perceived to be pillaging the country's mineral wealth. Seeing the writing on the wall, Frits and Henry had summarily retired from the mineral prospecting business and each bought large tracts of land in order to try their hands at farming. Frits had at first considered going back to South Africa where the whites were still respected, but Henry had convinced his friend to stay – where else could they afford to buy such fertile land at such low prices? Frits settled in Mukushi District while Henry and his wife Laura bought land in Makeni, just south of Lusaka. Frits soon discovered that commercial farming was not an easy pursuit. Unlike the bohemian lifestyle of a prospector, a farmer, besides capital, required discipline, patience, and an ability to plan ahead – virtues which he lacked. Frits attempted to grow maize, soybeans and even tobacco but each season he would fall victim to the unpredictable rains which devastated his harvest. Desperate to reverse the situation, Frits took out a bank loan using his farm as surety in order to install an expensive irrigation system. It was a huge gamble, one that ultimately failed leaving him profoundly in debt.

Five months earlier ...

Mukushi District

February, 1979

Henry and Frits sat next to each other on two wicker chairs on Frits' porch one afternoon. They looked out into the garden, a bank of *masuku* trees dotted a small bluff overgrown with shrubs. Frits had tried to keep as much of the indigenous foliage on his farm as possible. It reminded him of the times when he led a Spartan life working for the prospecting company, Chesterman and Oakley. He recalled when, in their younger days, he and Henry would spend weeks on end deep in the bush searching for mineral deposits. He missed that life.

Henry had arrived in Mukushi earlier that day for a short visit on his way back from a business trip up north. The two men had spent much of the day drinking and reminiscing about the old days but even through the levity, Henry had sensed the weight of something unsaid. Despite their long twenty-year friendship, there remained a rivalry between them – to admit to Henry that he was on the cusp of losing everything was something Frits just couldn't do. It was hard for a proud man like him to admit failure, although he had not slept well for months, tormented by his thoughts. However, as the afternoon wore on, alcohol began to loosen his tongue and quail his inhibitions, until finally he told his story.

For a moment, Henry sat silently in his chair before reaching for a cigarette from the packet on the side table between them. He lit it and cupping his hands together, he pulled hard. "Well, what a right mess you've got yourself into Fritsy old chap. … What do you propose to do about it?" As if spilling the beans had both relieved him, and removed the last of his pride, Frits was slumped in his chair. He rubbed the back of his neck. He owed money and lots of it. The way things were going, his farm would be repossessed by the bank before year's end and there seemed to be nothing he could do about it.

Henry swirled the scotch in his hand before throwing it down his throat in one gulp. Taking a long hard pull at his cigarette, he blew into the air above his head. Then he leaned forward slowly until his face was just inches away from Frits. "Look around you old chap." He said in a measured tone. "Is this what you want for yourself? … Let's be honest Fritsy, you and I both know we have no business pretending to be commercial farmers. I realised it from the moment Laura and I bought that farm in Makeni. It was her idea to settle down and build a life for ourselves. It was a romantic idea. Farming is tough and we've never really had either the know-how or the capital." Henry gazed reflectively into the distance. "For years we've barely made ends meet, after paying for the feed and the workers' wages, there was hardly anything left. About two years ago, we came close to losing it all. At that point, I told Laura we needed to sell the damned place but … you know how stubborn she can be … she just wouldn't hear of it." He sighed and shook his head. "I knew we couldn't survive one more year like that and so I decided something had to be done. That was when I made my decision to go back to what I know best … you know, use the skills we learned all those years ago."

Frits shook his head in resignation. "But you know there's no way a *muzungu's* gonna get a permit to go mining in this country … the *bledy* greedy politicians have it all rigged … they're *bledy* making themselves rich, hand over fist, while talking about independence this, independence that …equal opportunity … but let a *muzungu* like you or me try to get a permit, hey? …No chance!"

Henry stabbed what was left of his cigarette into an ashtray. He looked up calmly. "Well, that's what you have to decide my friend, do you give up and let them take advantage while you quietly follow the rules and end up walking the streets with a begging bowl? Or do you do something about it? … I chose to do something."

Frits turned his head. "What do you mean?" Henry sat back, a smile lurking. Frits looked over his shoulder towards the house to see if his houseboy was within earshot. He waited for a few seconds as the young man stretched a checked cloth over a table in the room behind them. "What do you mean?… Illegal mining?" Henry didn't respond but the expression in his eyes told Frits all he needed to know.

"But how?... I hear the military have clamped down on illegal mining … soldiers everywhere … they're *bledy* shooting people on sight."

Henry remained evasive. "Oh there are ways, if you know the right people … let's just say I've been able to secure a little something for our future."

"And Laura? … What does she …"

Henry placed a fresh stick in the side of his mouth and lit it. Blowing smoke through his nostrils, he shook his head. "When the time is right, I'll tell her …. She won't like it, but what's done is done … she'll eventually come around."

"But how? … How long? How did you do it?" Frits asked.

"A little over a year … I know some people … being a 'National Hero' does have its perks. As you rightly put it, many of these politicians have been flouting the rules, carrying out mining activities and pocketing the proceeds. I was approached to lend my expertise in prospecting … they offered to pay me in stones … so, for a small cut here and there, I've been lending a hand … you know showing them the best sites to excavate and so on. It's taken a little while but I've managed to put aside enough to make sure we don't lose the farm." He turned to face Frits directly. "If you're up for it, old chap, I can put in a word for you … just let me know and I'll see what I can do."

Frits rubbed his chin. He looked up and saw his houseboy leaving through the back door of the kitchen holding a basin heaped with damp garments. The young man crossed the threshold into the garden and began to hang towels on a clothes line. Frits thought about what life would be like without maids and servants waiting on him hand and foot – he could scarcely imagine it. As he leant back in quiet contemplation he realised that there was no greater fear within him than the thought of being a poor white man in a black man's country.

The news of Henry's debilitating stroke came barely a week afterwards. It arrived like a heavily laden train crashing through a stanchion. Frits could not help but rue his misfortune. Not only was his friend Henry in hospital fighting for his life, Frits' hopes of extricating himself from his financial malaise had been instantly dashed. It is oft said that a man walks in darkness while his destiny approaches him. Indeed, Frits could feel the immanency of his demise. That very day he travelled to Lusaka to find Laura sitting by her husband's bedside holding his hand. Her eyes were puffy from crying. She immediately perked up with a smile through her tears as she watched Frits entering the ward. There were beds on either side of the aisle filled with patients and visiting relatives. Henry was near the entrance, next to an open window which offered a welcome breeze. She wrapped her arms around Frits' expansive mid-riff pressing herself against him. He could feel her tender sobs. "Oh Fritsy … I'm so glad you've come … I'm so …" He tightened his grip around her and they stood in each other's embrace both wondering whether or not Henry would pull through.

Frits stayed at the Hinckley's homestead in Makeni during those trying first few days when they didn't know if Henry would survive. He proved a godsend to Laura who had to make the daily trek into town each morning to Henry's bedside in hospital, only returning after dark. Frits would stay behind for most of the day and took care of sundries around the farm. In truth, Nawakwi the housemaid, the driver Elijah Nkole and Bashi Joshua the foreman, were able to dispense their charges without supervision. They ensured the farm continued to run relatively smoothly in Laura's absence. On the mornings when Frits was left alone to watch Nawakwi sweeping the floors, he wondered if Henry's small horde of emeralds was hidden somewhere in the house?

Early one morning as Laura prepared to leave the house, she sat Frits down at the dining room table. Nawakwi had prepared the morning tea as always and left it on a covered tray. As she sipped her tea, Laura explained how the takings from the livestock pens had fallen woefully short of expectations for the past two months and there was currently not enough cash to settle the money owed to Ifundo Milling Limited, the supplier of their livestock feed. Ifundo had been threatening to cease supply until all outstanding invoices were settled. Laura appeared overwhelmed, with Henry fighting for his life in hospital and now this? "Henry said he was sorting it out but then everything happened … we can't afford for them to stop supplying us with feed …we wouldn't last a week … we just wouldn't … I …" Laura sounded exasperated and near to tears. Frits reached for her hand.

"Don't worry, Laura … focus on Henry, I'll sort it out, I'll go there today and speak to them. It'll be all right, hey … listen to me … it'll be all right, you'll see."

✳

Frits and the driver, Elijah Nkole, arrived at Ifundo Milling Limited just before noon that morning. The guard opened the wire gate and stood aside in a clumsy salute as they drove in. There was a parking bay right in front of a small office to their left and they parked in an open space next to three other vehicles.

"You can wait here," Frits said as he stepped out of the car. Walking towards the office building, he could see a large storage area with corrugated roofing sheets to his right. There was a loading bay adjacent to the storage area and three shirtless men covered in dust heaving sacks of grain into the back of a van.

A diminutive white lady was sitting in the front office, Frits couldn't quite place her accent – Greek or Cypriot perhaps? He imagined she was related to the owner, so he spoke politely. He asked to see the Managing Director. He said he had some important business to discuss concerning Hinckley Farm. The Director was out at lunch, the woman said, and would be returning at around one o'clock. Frits was free to wait or come back later. She offered him a cup of tea but he declined, deciding to wait outside.

After smoking underneath the shade of an awning for a little while, Frits took a final pull of his cigarette before crushing it underfoot. An impatient man, he hated waiting. Then his mind would crowd with worry; he needed diversion, he began to walk. He made his way towards the parked vehicle where Elijah was seated with the windows open. "I'll be right back." Frits said. He soon reached the perimeter gate where the dozing sentry immediately sparked to life and rose to his feet in salute.

"Afternoon *bwana*!"

Frits nodded as he stepped outside the premises. Tall grass and shrubs stretched into the distance on either side of the gravel road that let from the main gate to Kafue Road. Intrigued by a narrow footpath to his side, Frits made his way down it. As he walked, all he could think about was how the fortunes of white people like him had changed for the worse. Ever since Independence, the system had seemed rigged against whites. He knew it was an obsession, and one that recurred whenever he had too much time on his hands, but he still felt angry and bitter. His mind whirred down its usual trajectory when suddenly he was interrupted by a familiar odour from some nearby bushes – *Dagga!*

He paused, looking carefully into the bush and saw a shirtless man leaning against the trunk of a tree. Frits moved closer and the man quickly rose to his feet. He was tall and lanky, his eyes glassy and red, lowering his head, he shifted nervously before hiding his hand behind his back.

"What do you have there?" Frits asked. The man cowered at the question. "Don't be shy, hey … what's your name?"

"Mu… Mu … Mutamina, *bwana*." The man mumbled.

"What are you doing here?" Frits asked but the man did not answer. "You work here?" Frits pointed behind him. The young man kept his eyes to the ground. "Answer me man …" The young man eventually nodded slowly. Frits eyed him from head to foot, his arms were ashen from working in the mill. Frits spoke evenly. "So, you come here to smoke *dagga*, hey? Do you understand that if I tell your *bwana*, you could lose your job?" Silence. The young man stood still. The distinct earthen aroma of the herb wafted into the air – it had been a while since he had smoked a good joint. It brought back memories of the bohemian life which he'd once led. He extended his hand. Mutamina, gingerly handed him the smouldering joint. Frits held it between his two fingers as he savoured the rich aroma, before bringing it towards his parted lips and inhaled deeply. Two down-and-outs together' he thought, as he sat himself down beside Paul.

When Henry eventually regained consciousness days later, he was unable to speak or walk. Still, Laura managed to convince the doctors to discharge him from hospital, arguing that his chances of making a recovery were surely better in the familiar surroundings of his home, rather than in an overcrowded hospital ward. Frits watched as his friend was finally brought home – a shadow of himself. Whether he would ever be able to speak or walk again was uncertain but Laura maintained hope. Two weeks later, Frits returned to his farm in Mukushi with his fortunes unchanged and bereft of ideas on how to save himself. It would be another two months before he would see Henry and Laura again.

Kwacha Motel

Frits opened his eyes to the sound of gusting wind and a vehicle outside of his window. He had fallen asleep in his chair. The television set was still on but there were only black and white pixels shimmering on the screen. He lowered his feet from the coffee table and checked the time. He had been asleep for close to three hours. Lifting himself out of his chair, he fell flat on top of his bed. The room was dimly lit from a security lamp outside the window. Frits stared at the ceiling, his thoughts again returning to the last time he had visited Laura and Henry Hinckley.

Three months earlier...
April, 1979
Hinckley Farm, Makeni

After Laura and Frits had returned to the farmhouse, Frits sat himself down on the sofa while Laura and Nawakwi went to attend to Henry in the bedroom. He lit a cigarette and looked up at a copper plaque with an African rhino positioned in the centre of the longest wall between various framed photographs: Henry and Laura in their younger days gazing dotingly at each other, and so on. Frits felt his palms begin to sweat. The truth was that he had not travelled solely to check on his ailing friend – no, there was another more selfish reason for his visit. Following Laura's letter informing him that Henry had made 'significant' strides in his recovery, Frits had hurried over hoping that Henry would be well enough to talk. Frits was desperate, every passing day brought him closer to financial ruin. He needed more information about the gemstone business, and who Henry's contacts were.

He heard Laura's voice echoing against the walls, "I have a surprise for you honey, you won't believe whose here." It was surprising how often people raised their voices when speaking to the infirm, even if they were not deaf.

Frits rose to his feet as Laura entered the room holding a box of tissues, in her wake came Henry being wheeled in by Nawakwi. His heart sank, how his old friend had withered. The 'significant' strides in recovery he had hoped for were barely visible. Henry's skin was wrinkled and pale, he had lost most of his hair, and the left of his face appeared to have fallen in. He had aged decades in a matter of weeks.

Laura mustered a smile, perhaps she could sense Frits' disappointment. "Look who's here, Henry!" She said a little too loudly. "I really wanted to surprise you, love." Henry stared blankly at his feet unaware of his surroundings. Frits stepped forward and lowered himself to his haunches.

"You old hyena! Stop pretending and get out of that chair, hey! ...I know all you want is to be pampered by women, huh!" Frits attempted to lighten the mood. He searched Henry's face for a response, but it remained blank. Dribble ran down his chin.

✳

That afternoon, after several failed attempts at a conversation, Henry was wheeled back to his bedroom while Laura and Frits made their way onto the verandah. At Laura's instruction, Nawakwi brought out a bottle of Merlot for her and Jameson whisky for Frits on a silver tray which she put on the table. The two friends worn out by immediate emotion, found relief in walking down memory lane. They talked about when Henry and Laura arrived as newlyweds from England, how they had stayed in a small room in Frits' three-bedroomed bungalow. Laura had wondered why Frits was not married and why there seemed to be no prospect in sight. Of course, that was before she knew him well, before they had really spent time together. In the years that followed Laura would realise that Frits was not the settling down type – no, he preferred his freedom.

As it began to grow dark, Laura called Nawakwi from inside the house. She appeared instantly as if she had been waiting in the wings for her madam to summon her. She stood in the doorway a distance away, lowering herself respectfully. "Yes, ma." She said.

"Please be a darling and check on *bwana* Hinckley, will you?" The housemaid nodded. "Make sure he eats something … I don't want him to lose any more weight." Nawakwi nodded again. "I'll put together some left overs for Fritsy and I."

"Yes ma. Thank you ma."

Laura turned to Frits. "You don't mind that, do you?"

Frits lifted his glass. "Ah – you know me, hey. I'll eat anything!"

They sat for some time in the cool night breeze as a chorus of crickets competed with the sound of rustling leaves in the trees beyond the house. Laura ran her fingers through her hair and stared into the kerosene lamp placed between them. She began to tell a story about how she had visited the small breeze block homes belonging to her farmworkers a few days earlier. She rambled on about how poor they were and how she wished she could do more for them. Frits peered into his glass, he had lost count of the number of glasses he had downed. His thoughts drifted back to his farm and all the money he owed and how the whole thing was suffocating him like a noose tightening around his neck. He wished he had made the decision in '64 to leave and return to South Africa or even Southern Rhodesia. At least they had not been ruined by these corrupt and incompetent black majority governments spawning across the continent like an infestation. But it was too late now, he had invested all his money and more on his farm in Mukushi and now he was about to lose everything. For a moment there seemed to have been a life line, one last hope of a reprieve but alas, this had turned to ashes once he learned of Henry's stroke. He looked up at Laura, her lips were moving but he couldn't hear what she was saying. Then, he slowly lowered his glass and stopped her in mid-sentence. "I know about the emeralds, Laura."

Laura covered her mouth, fighting back tears. "…Oh Fritsy … I didn't know … Honestly, I didn't know that things were so bad … surely there's a way out of it …they can't just take away your farm … everything that you've worked so hard to build… surely not."

"They *bledy* can and they will." Frits said, frustration seeping into his voice. He had just finished explaining his situation to her, how desperate he was, how Henry had promised to help him and how in an instant his hopes had been dashed. Laura sat silently for what seemed like an eternity. What was she thinking? Why the hesitation? The reluctance to help him? He was not asking for a hand out – no, all he was asking for was a loan which he would pay back in full when he had the money. In fact, the way he saw it, he would be doing her a favour. What did Laura know about gemstones or how to find buyers? With Henry incapacitated, he would take care of everything and make sure she got enough money to look after Henry and the farm. In turn, he would be able to stave off the hounds. It was a win-win for everyone involved, surely she could see that!

"I… I … I can't, Fritsy… it's … it's just not right …it's …"

Frits was hot around the collar, he could scarcely hold his composure any longer. "Not right? … Not right? … not right for who, hey? …For *bledy* who? Tell me!"

Laura raised her hand, showing Frits her palm. "I understand you're upset, Fritsy, but that's no reason to speak to me in that manner." She said briskly. "I knew nothing about those stones until the day Henry came to talk to me about what he'd done. For one whole year he had gone behind my back to do this … this thing. Smuggling on behalf of crooks! He kept it from me knowing full well I would never have stood for it. He knows how I feel about such things … it's not right, not right at all." She swallowed hard. Frits attempted to speak but she cut him off. "That day … the day he came to me and told me what he had done… we argued. It was … it was the biggest fight we've had in all our time together… we said things … I … I said things to him…" She wiped away a tear from her cheek. "… that was the night he had the stroke."

Frits held his head in his hands. "Laura, you can't blame yourself for what happened to Henry, it's not your fault."

She shook her head. "Fritsy, I blame those blasted stones. If he hadn't gone out to …"

"But what's done is done, Laura. You have them now and if we play our cards right, those stones can sort out all of our …"

"I won't do it Fritsy … I will not. I would never be able to live with myself." There was a steely resolve in her voice. This was the stubborn Laura of old.

Frits implored her but deep inside he knew that her mind was made and there were no words that could persuade her. "But, Laura, be rational about it. What do you intend to do with them, hey … *bledy* give them away?"

"I don't know, but what I will not do is have us benefit from ill-gotten gains!"

25

A Night in the Township

11:03 p.m.

A few kilometres south of Kapiri Mposhi ...

Max and Ronald sped through the night in their Land Rover heading northwards to Kapiri Mposhi. Upon returning from Chimutengo Prison, both men had briefly stopped at their homes to pack a few clothes before heading out to Kapiri – there was no time to waste as the suspects in custody had to be interrogated. It was a four-hour drive from the capital, on a single lane road. Max replayed the events of the day in his mind. He regretted having left home under such circumstances – so much unsaid, matters of the heart unresolved. He sighed sadly, it would have to wait. Right now, there was tremendous pressure to bring this murder investigation to a successful conclusion, and he could feel the stress.

Max thought about the telephone call he had received while they were in Warden Bwembya's office. The officer on the call had told him about how three men in a blue Fiat sedan had been stopped at a police checkpoint approximately two kilometres south of Kapiri Mposhi. The men were asked to show their identification papers but the routine stop quickly turned deadly when one of them fled from the vehicle into the night. Warning shots were fired but the man did not stop and was gunned down. Max rued the loss of a life. It needn't have been this way. All too often, it seemed that young officers were far too quick to employ deadly force. The two other men were now in police custody and had apparently confessed to being involved in a farm invasion in the Makeni area. Max cringed as he imaged the coercive tactics that had most surely been employed to bring the suspects to talk – didn't they realise that if beaten enough, a suspect will admit to anything?

Max stretched his neck. He had been driving for a while and was beginning to tire. He cracked the window open and a stream of fresh air rushed inside the car. The sudden noise made Ronald open his eyes and sit up in his seat.

"How much longer?" Ronald asked.

"We should be arriving in another ten to fifteen minutes." Max rolled up the window again. He stared ahead and remembered that there was a message that Jennifer had left for him about a friend of the Hinckleys, who had wanted to see him. He would have to call her and tell her to have him see one of the other detectives if he showed up again at the station.

11:11 p.m.

Kwacha Motel, Lusaka

Frits sat on the side of the bed and placed his face into his hands. A torrent of emotion making him weep like a child. He hadn't meant for things to turn out this way, but there was nothing he could do to bring back Laura and Henry. He rose from the bed and made his way into the tiny hotel bathroom. He slumped over the sink. There was a dirt-stained crack in the ceramic that ran from the edge all the way down into the drain. He turned the hot water tap but no water came out. He then opened the cold water spigot and a weak stream sputtered out. He watched as the brown liquid turned translucent before splashing his face with his hands. Frits straightened himself and stared into the mirror. Laura and Henry had been killed but he could still save his farm if only he could get his hands on the emeralds. He needed to speak with the detective in charge of the case. He had to know what the police knew. Were they in possession of the stones? And if so, could he convince the detective in charge to release them to him? In his mind *'they'*, all black men, were corruptible when it came down to it, for the right price he could get his way.

Three months earlier...

April, 1979

Hinckley Farm, Makeni

Frits felt anger, confusion and betrayal as he left Hinckley Farm that night, but above all he was afraid. Indeed, there was no greater fear within him than the thought of being a poor white man in a black man's country. Following their conversation, Laura had retired to bed leaving him sitting out on the veranda. After a while, he had risen from his chair and walked to the front of the house. He was met by Chanter and Whisky, the two boerboels, sniffing at his ankles and knees. He lowered himself and stroked them for a moment – if only human beings were as loyal and compliant as animals. There was no one outside. It was dark and he could not see the livestock pens nor the workers homes which stood a fair distance away. Frits slowly made his way to his car and opened the door. He sat in the driver's seat for a while, his emotions shifting back and forth between anger and despair. Soon he found himself driving on the main road heading southwards with no particular destination in mind.

He must have driven for several minutes before turning off the main road onto a gravel track flanked on either side by makeshift homes. He was not sure where it would lead but he kept on driving. Not too long afterwards, he arrived at a clearing where in front of him was a building made of concrete blocks. He could see a dim light through the windows and there was a small group of men gathered outside on wooden stools with beer bottles in hand. He guessed it was some sort of township shebeen. There was but one old vehicle parked next to the building, a sure sign that most people had arrived on foot. Frits sat silently, the engine rumbling, headlights illuminating the night. The group of men sitting outside shielded their eyes from the blinding light unsure of what to make of the vehicle stationed in front of them. Finally, Frits stepped out of the car.

A burly white man in a township tavern – Frits stood out like a sore thumb. Impervious to the curious stares, he perched himself in a hidden corner and ordered a drink.

✳

Frits had been sitting quietly out of sight in the back of the tavern drinking his beer – township bars rarely stock imported whisky, when suddenly he heard raised voices and the sound of wooden furniture screeching against the concrete floor. He raised his head and saw a group of men on their feet towards the back of the room. He watched carefully, unsure of what to do. Yes, he was a large brawny man who ordinarily fancied himself against anyone in a scrap, but in this instance he recognised that he was a singular white man in unfamiliar surroundings. The melee quickly spilled into the night. Frits rose to his feet, grabbing his bottle, he made his way through the doors and was soon hovering in the dark behind the circle that now surrounded two brawlers, trying not to attract attention. One of the men was of medium height with significant heft, the other tall and lanky. Frits immediately recognised the lanky young man - it was one of the workers from Ifundo Milling, the one he had found smoking *dagga* a few months ago when he last stayed at Hinckley Farm. The small crowd of spectators was cheering and egging the two men on. The hefty fellow pulled his right arm from the other man's clutches and cocked his fist. He threw a punch which landed in the side of his opponent's face. The sound made Frits grimace, he wondered what had triggered the scuffle but he was unwilling to step in. Astonishingly, the tall young man held his ground returning with a barrage of blows which sent his adversary tumbling to the ground. The crowd erupted in cheers as the lanky fellow moved forward but before he could finish his adversary off, a smartly dressed man stepped out of the crowd into the circle. "What is this, eh?" He yelled. "I won't have this sort of thing in my bar! ... Not in my bar! ... I'll have the whole lot of you arrested, eh? *Basopo*! I'll call the police and *onse imwe* you'll be sleeping *muma* cells *cabe!*" The crowd sobered instantly. He turned to the lanky man, whose chest was still heaving and his nostrils flaring. "And you ... Mutamina ... is it not enough that you owe me money for rent?... Now you come here to cause me trouble?... I should kick you and your family out! Get out of my sight... I don't want trouble here, you understand?" Paul Mutamina retreated into the night as the small crowd began to make its way back into the building.

✳

Morning arrived with the sound of Nawakwi sweeping the area outside his window. Frits rolled to his side and lifted a pillow to cover his head. His throat was dry, and his head still groggy from all the alcohol he had consumed the previous night. He could scarcely remember how he had made it back to Hinckley Farm. He gritted his teeth as he involuntarily recalled his last conversation with Laura. Her intransigence had become an obsession. How could she refuse to see reason? She could see how desperate he was and how selling those gemstones was the only thing that made sense for both of them. And she was a friend! It took him a moment to finally sit up on the side of the bed. He looked at his watch, it was almost ten o'clock in the morning. Laura would already be out of the house – there was no such thing as a late morning on a farm.

Nawakwi asked him what he wanted for breakfast but he had no appetite for anything, instead he downed two large glasses of water and slowly made his way outside. It was a beautiful day, the sun high in the sky. Frits lit a cigarette and stared into the distance towards one of the livestock pens. A team of workers were busy clearing out one of the sheds to lay fresh woodchips for a new batch of chicks. This was it, life on a farm – slow, deliberate, regimented and uninspiring.

A white van appeared in the driveway, Frits immediately recognised as a delivery van from Ifundo Milling. Two men sat inside the van and perched in the back, atop a stack of brown sacks, was Paul Mutamina. The vehicle stopped a few feet from one of the pens as the driver adjusted gear and reversed. When the back of the van was almost underneath the covered structure, the two men in the vehicle disembarked. They walked into the pen leaving Paul sitting in the back. Frits watched him from a distance and in that moment a thought came to him, clear as day – there was one last option which could save him from financial ruin.

26

The Story of Paul Mutamina

11:24 p.m.

Kapiri Mposhi

Max and Ronald reached a police checkpoint on the outskirts of Kapiri Mposhi. Two armed policemen hovered next to the vehicle as Max lowered his window. They had clearly read the 'ZP' Zambia Police number plate at the front of the car.

"Evening officer." Max said.

"*Sah*!" One of the officers said upon seeing Max's identification card. He straightened his back with his arms to his side in deference to the superior rank held by the man driving.

"We're from Lusaka Central … we're investigating an urgent case … we received a call from Kapiri Central that there was a shooting somewhere here last night and two suspects are in custody?"

"*Sah* – yes *sah*! Three men *sah*, just here *sah*." The uniformed officer pointed in the general area.

"I'm Detective Chanda and this is Detective Siatwinda." Ronald lowered his head in the car and gave a nod. "Central station is where?" Max asked. The officer gave directions, a rifle in his right hand.

When they reached the Station, the two detectives were promptly led to the holding cell behind a padlocked metal gate. The 'cell' was one small space with a tiny nook for the prisoners to relieve themselves – it wreaked of excrement. A young officer fiddled with a set of keys before unlocking the gate.

"Mutamina!" The officer yelled. "Paul Mutamina!"

The prisoner looked older than he had appeared in the photograph that Max and Ronald had seen of him at Chimutengo Prison. He sat on the concrete floor of the interrogation room with wrists and feet shackled. He cast a forlorn figure – barefooted, shirtless and sweaty. So much had transpired in the months since he had been released, so many setbacks, which had led him to where he sat now on a cold stone floor.

Max stood above him and laid his hand over his shoulder. "Mutamina … you need to tell us everything you know … everything … from the beginning."

Eight months ago …

December, 1978

Chimutengo Prison

Paul Mutamina was released eighteen months early from Chimutengo on account of his good behaviour. He left on a blistering hot afternoon in December 1978. His wife, Judy, was waiting for him underneath the shade of a mango tree, a few yards in front of the warden's office, where visitors typically gathered to see the inmates. Men, women and children would wait, sometimes for hours, to be called through the visitor's gate at the discretion of the guards on duty. Family members sat sullenly with their cooked food in covered metal plates, waiting anxiously to feed someone they loved. It was always a gamble as to whether or not the food would reach the intended recipients. The guards would habitually hijack the meals under the guise of 'illegal contraband' and consume it themselves. Even when food did make it past the guards' greedy clutches, it would invariably have to be shared among dozens of famished inmates.

Judy stood up when she saw her husband making his way past the iron gates manned by a uniformed sentry. Paul looked gaunt, his cheeks were hollow and his shoulders pointed. She felt the child to her side grab her *chitenge*. It was as if the child could sense its mother's anxiety. In truth, Judy could not quite put her finger on what she was feeling – elation … apprehension. She was glad to have her husband back, yet she had grown accustomed to life without him and was uneasy about the impending changes, his presence would inevitably demand. She would again have to get accustomed to his presence, his voice, his touch, the feeling of him breathing on top of her – the things a dutiful wife must do. Judy also worried about how their now four-year-old daughter, Chiko, would respond to having a new face in their midst, a face she had only encountered in moments whenever they visited the prison. All this occupied her mind but what concerned her the most was whether or not the good part of Paul would still be present after his stint in prison. She had heard stories about how prison changed men, extinguishing the good and bringing out the worst in them.

Paul crossed the threshold and soon met his wife in the middle of the dusty driveway which led from the office buildings to the main gate of the prison. His forehead glistened with perspiration in the sunlight. Judy laid a soft palm on his arm and asked him how he was doing. His eyes fled from her gaze and landed on his four year old daughter who was now clasping her mother's hand. "Chiko …" He said opening his arms, but the child pressed herself even more tightly against her mother's leg.

Judy patted her daughter gently before looking back up to Paul. "We should go *bashi* Chiko. We have a long journey." Glancing in the direction of the main gate, she could see two guards watching them carefully as if waiting for the opportunity to lock Paul up again.

They walked for close to an hour on a well-trodden dirt path before hitching a ride on a bus which would drop them off along the main tarred road on the outskirts of the Makeni farming area. Husband, wife and child then walked in near silence for another half hour until they arrived at a clearing where a number of single-roomed homes were clustered in a small enclave. This was where Judy had made her home for the past two and a half years since Paul had been away. Despite appeals from her family to move back to her village in Lundazi District, Judy had chosen to stay near to her husband. She had taken to making and selling charcoal. The work was hard – cutting down trees with an axe, her child strapped on her back. She would chop the logs into small pieces, and stack them inside a kiln made from moist red earth. When the charcoal was ready, she would gather it into mushroom shaped sacks to sell along the main road.

One thing about prison is that all decisions are made for you – when to eat, when to sleep, where and when you should work and for how long. With prison came a sense of anonymity that was strangely comforting – Paul could hide in it. However, in the outside world he was struggling to keep on the straight and narrow, the temptation to go get back into petty crime ever present. For some time, all that Paul could find was the occasional work as a day labourer on some of the nearby commercial farms. The work was back breaking and the wages paltry. He found that whenever a decent job was on offer, he would be immediately disqualified once they learned of his stint in prison for robbery. Finally, desperate to change his fortunes, he lied on an application form for a job as a general worker for a local milling company called, Ifundo Milling Limited, which supplied livestock feed to the local farms.

Paul noticed the vehicle parked on the side of the dirt track as he walked out of the pedestrian gate. The sentry slumped in the tiny guard house nodded at him as he glanced in his direction. He was one of the last few workers to leave as he had stayed behind to load the van for the next morning's deliveries.

From a distance, Paul could not tell if there was anyone inside the vehicle but as he drew nearer he recognised the *muzungu* sitting in the driver's seat. It was the same *muzungu* who had caught him smoking *dagga* two months earlier. His heart began to pound inside his chest. What was he doing here, what did he want? When Paul arrived within a few feet of the car, the white man lowered his window.

The *muzungu* said he wanted something from the farm. Something which belonged to him. Paul explained to the detectives. He said the owners of the farm had taken something from him and that he needed returned. The white man had said that he needed someone who could go in and get it from the house for he could not do so himself as he had had an argument with the owners of the farm. Paul's lips had quivered as Max and Ronald looked on attentively. Paul went on to say that he had had no choice in the matter for the *muzungu* had threatened to expose his *dagga* smoking to his *bwana* at Ifundo Milling Limited and that he would surely have lost his job. Paul had conveniently neglected to mention that the white man had enticed him with a wad of cash – more money than he had ever held in his hands before, with the promise of more to come if Paul could deliver the small package held in a safe somewhere in the house. The plan, as Paul explained, was to wait until the white man gave the word, he was to provide the exact time and day when the burglary was to take place – but he wanted to wait until the time was right. Max asked him to name the white man and what was hidden in the safe. Paul shook his head and said he did not know what was hidden in the safe, all he knew was the white man's name – *bwana* Frits. Max's back stiffened, he recognised the name, it was the same name on the note Jennifer had left for him in the office the previous day.

Detective Ronald Siatwinda had sighed heavily before speaking in a measured tone. "So you expect us to believe that it was some white man who told you to murder an innocent couple in order to obtain some unknown contraband?" Max was impressed by the restraint that his junior detective was exhibiting, perhaps he was learning that a good investigator needed to reign in their emotions in order to get to the facts. Mutamina shook his head.

"No, *sah* … no *sah* … it was not the plan to kill … to hurt anybody, *sah* … it was …" Paul's head fell into his palms and he wept like a child. The two detectives waited for his sobs to subside. Then he looked up at them, eyes bloodshot. "It was *ba* Amos … Amos Mushili."

❋

Three months earlier ...

April, 1979

Kabulonga, Lusaka

Paul signalled to the conductor to stop the mini-bus at the next stop. The bus soon veered off the tarmac and onto a dusty embankment where Paul angled past bodies until he was out of the vehicle. The young conductor stepped back into the doorframe and yelled out to a group of women across the street. "*Muleya?*" They shook their heads prompting the crusty-eyed conductor to tap the side of the bus and they were off again.

Paul searched the area in front of him: high fences, manicured lawns and lush flower beds. He was not used to being in such rich suburbs. He moved quickly past two yards with iron gates to his right. As he reached the third house, the gate opened allowing him a glimpse at a stately mansion nestled behind palm trees. This was worlds apart from his one-roomed shack in the township.

Several minutes later, Paul stood in front of a girdled fence. An elderly porter eyed him suspiciously. "*Ufuna andani?*" He asked.

"*Nifuna a* Amos Mushili." Paul replied. The guard asked several more questions concerning the nature of his visit, then after a short pause, he looked him over once more before opening. Paul was led along a neatly paved path which snaked around the main house to a guesthouse in the back. In Paul's eyes, the size of the guesthouse could have been many times the size of the biggest home in the township. The guard remained watching at a distance as Paul knocked on the front door.

It took several minutes before the door pulled open. The smell of *dagga* smoke immediately wafted into the air as Amos Mushili stood shirtless in the doorway wearing a pair of shorts that scarcely hid an erection. He cracked a smile. "Ah, if it isn't my dear old friend Mutamina. You have arrived at exactly the right time." Paul could hear female voices giggling in the background.

Paul had known he was in over his head. What the *muzungu* was proposing to do was grander and more audacious than anything he had been involved in before. Besides, his last attempt at larceny had landed him in prison for over two years. If he were to attempt something like that again, he would need help from someone more intelligent and more daring than him, someone who had guile and fortitude to attempt anything. He could think of none other than Amos Mushili.

❊

Once again, Paul had found himself on the wrong side of the law and he knew that he would pay dearly for it. Poor and illiterate, Paul now realised that he had fallen victim to the machinations of the white man and Amos Mushili. It was his desperation that had driven him to accept the job from *bwana* Frits to rob the farmhouse and retrieve a package for which he knew not the contents. Frits had not divulged what was hidden in the safe, nor its true value just that he was willing to pay handsomely for it. Looking back now, Paul felt a familiar sense of humiliation for not challenging the white man to tell him exactly what was in the little bag.

Paul tried to gather himself together while the two detectives mulled over his story. What pained him the most was the fact that Amos had betrayed him. Having declined to take on the job when initially approached, Amos had returned days later with a renewed interest in leading the charge to break into the white couple's farmhouse. Initially bewildered by the change in heart, Paul had nonetheless been relieved to let Amos assume the reins. The man had then smoothly explained a detailed plan about how they would execute the robbery and escape northwards to the Copperbelt where they would wait in hiding before delivering the white man's package. Once the *muzungu* had paid them, they agreed to split the money equally. How wrong he had been!

❊

Night of the Hinckley murders ...

The four men sat silently in the car as they pulled into the gravel track which led to Hinckley Farm. Amos Mushili turned off the lights to the vehicle, it was dark but he drove for several more metres using the distant light of the farmhouse as a guide. He eventually stopped the car and turned off the engine.

"This is as close as we can get without anyone noticing us." Amos declared. Each man gathered a weapon from his feet. There were two machetes and two crowbars. They stepped out of the vehicle, the air was still, it was unusual for the month of July when the winds could sometimes blow hard enough to fell trees. Perhaps it was an omen of the events that would shortly unfold.

Paul turned to Amos. "*Ba* Amos, you brought the poison for the dogs?" The white man had told Paul that the Hinckleys had two dogs and that they would need to be put to sleep before they could enter the house. When Paul had relayed this to Amos, Amos had volunteered to bring a special drug which, he claimed, would knock them out cold. He had said it was a drug which he had used on dates with women before. Paul had simply nodded – he was not familiar with such things but trusted that *ba* Amos knew more than he did.

"Don't worry about the dogs ... I'll handle them." Amos was confidence itself.

They moved on foot towards the main house, past a set of livestock pens on either side of the road. The smell of manure wafted into the night. As they reached within yards of the house, a dog began to bark. Paul heard one of the men behind him breathe heavily. Then Musa yelped as a dog leapt forward and bit at his leg pulling at his trousers. The mutt growled as it shook from side to side. Within an instant, a second canine was upon them. Paul attempted to beat it back but then he heard it squeal in pain. Amos had struck it across the head with his machete! He raised his weapon again and dealt it a fatal blow. Without hesitation, he turned and struck the second boerbel and the night fell into an eerie silence. In that moment, Paul knew that he had made a terrible mistake in involving Amos Mushili.

DAY 4
Monday, July 23ʳᵈ 1979

27

All Hands on Deck

7:32 a.m.

Lusaka Central Police Station

The telephone rang at exactly seven thirty-two in the morning. Jennifer Yumbe knew this because she had just sat down at her desk.

"Good morning ... sir? Yes, sir." She picked up a pen and opened a notepad in front of her. She nodded her head as she scribbled down the instructions from her boss, Detective Maxwell Chanda. Her curvy calligraphy lagged behind her eager wrist as she raced across the page. "Yes ... yes sir, yes sir, uh-huh, yes sir." She paused before opening her diary and flicking through the pages. "His name was ... Mr Frits ... Frits ... Hub-er... let me spell it for you H-U-B-E-R-C-H-T ... yes, a white man. No he did not leave an address. ... Yes, I will inform Chief Mbewe as soon as he calls or comes into the station ...yes sir, thank you sir." She held the receiver against her ear for a few seconds longer before placing it gently back on its cradle. Picking up her notepad she read over her hurried notes:

> *'Dangerous suspect on the run ... name – Amos Mushili – Search ... parent's home ... Plot 216 Kaizer Road ... Kabulonga – Call Chief Mbewe ... Alert all units ... if* muzungu *comes – DO NOT let him leave – Search all hotels ...'*

Jennifer shivered as she read the message. The situation had changed very quickly; her boss had sounded rushed and determined. He said that he was at Kapiri Mposhi Central Police Station with Detective Siatwinda, following a lead to the Hinckley case. He had made several failed attempts to get a hold of Chief Mbewe on the phone and he needed her to pass on the message to him urgently.

✳

8:59 a.m.

Kabulonga, Lusaka

An armoured truck pulled up in front of an iron girdled gate. Half a dozen men in military fatigues jumped out of the back of the vehicle and demanded that the elderly sentry let them in.

Four of the uniformed men fanned out on the expansive grounds clasping their machine guns. They trampled over cannas and gladioli lining the tarred driveway. The rest of the men jumped back into the back of the truck and drove up to the stately two-storey mansion.

In no time at all, the men were standing at the front stoep. One of the men hammered his knuckles against the wooden door while another hovered behind him holding his gun. The impatient rasping at the door echoed through the corridors of the plush villa as they waited with scowls etched on their faces. Moments later, an elderly maid in a plain grey dress and apron opened the door.

"Mushili Amos, *alikuti?*" The soldier said gruffly. The woman shook her head.

"Who's inside?" The soldier demanded.

Trembling, she replied, "*Ni a madamu chabe.*" They pushed her side and rushed up the carpeted stairway leaving scuff marks with their dirty boots. They entered the first room at the top of the corridor, it was a bathroom and it was empty. They quickly moved on, but before they could open the adjacent door, they heard a sound coming from the end of the corridor. Fleet footed, they moved forward, their guns raised. Pausing at the door, they exchanged glances before kicking it open.

"*Hiyeee mayo nafwa!*" A buxom middle-aged woman screamed, raising her arms in surrender. The towel that had been wrapped round her fell to the floor. Humiliated, she bent and grabbed it, moaning with anxiety.

"Mushili … Where's he?"

Tears began to roll down the woman's face. She was too frightened to respond.

Outside, the other officers had entered the guest house and were searching it from top to bottom. They would soon discover that Amos Mushili had been gone for several days and nobody knew where he was.

9:05 a.m.

Kwacha Motel, Lusaka

Frits rubbed a damp towel over his face. He pressed the warm cloth against his cheeks for a few seconds before dropping it into the basin. He stared into the bathroom mirror. There were bags underneath his eyes; a three-day beard covered his chin. The facts were inescapable, his selfishness had led to the death of two of his closest friends. He felt sick. Murder had never been part of the plan: never. He had specifically instructed Paul Mutamina that the Hinckleys were not to be harmed in any way. All they needed to do was to find a small package, which was probably hidden in a safe, and bring it to him. How could he have misjudged the man so badly?

Frits pulled a clean shirt from his duffel bag. He put on his khaki shorts, his stout thighs boasting a thick mat of orange hair. Once he was dressed, he left his room for the main lobby. A man toiling away with a hoe in a flower bed stopped and greeted him with a soft respectful clap of his hands. Frits nodded in acknowledgement. When he arrived at the lobby, he saw two suited men at the porter's desk. He heard a snippet of their conversation, something about the strong winds the previous night. As soon as he walked through the archway, they stopped and greeted him, both men moving aside to make way for him – these small gestures always escaped Frits, who was oblivious to the courtesies that he enjoyed simply by virtue of his skin colour. He waited as the porter turned from the men he had been serving to give him priority, turning off the radio on the shelf behind him as he did so.

"Wait!" Frits said suddenly. "Turn up the volume!"

There was a crackle of static before the voice of a male newscaster filled the airwaves. " … to repeat … police have apprehended two suspects in the murder of Laura and Henry Hinckley of Makeni. One suspect was shot and killed while attempting to flee a police checkpoint in Kapiri Mposhi. Police are on the hunt for more suspects believed to be on the run. On other news …" Frits felt the blood draining from his head and his knees growing weak. Everything was unravelling in front of him … what did the police know? Were they now searching for him too?

28

Footprints

The midday sun burned against the backs of the two shirtless captives sitting on the floor of the open van. Musa and Paul rocked from side to side with each bump in the gravel road under the watchful eyes of two uniformed officers wielding rifles. Plumes of dust rose from the earth as they channeled deeper into the country away from the main road. Every few minutes Max would hear a thump on the roof and he would stop the vehicle. Each time, an officer would lean forward and relay a new set of directions given to him by either Paul or Musa. "Are you sure?" The officer would yell before placing the sole of his boot against his hapless captives who were trying desperately to retrace the journey they had taken a few nights before. "Left *apa*? … speak up, *kamani* … speak up!"

Given what the two men had revealed at the station, Max had reasoned that it made sense to take a team of officers back to where the men had been holed up and then fan out from there to see if they could track down Amos Mushili and hopefully rescue the hostage he had taken – that is if the hostage was still alive. From everything Max had seen, Mushili sounded like a ruthless character who cared little about the lives of others. It seemed possible that Mushili could still be hiding somewhere in the woods waiting for the right moment to make his move.

Max had tried to call Chief Mbewe several times that morning but had failed to reach him. He now hoped that his secretary, Jennifer Yumbe, would deliver his message to the Chief so that a Special Forces unit could be dispatched to search Mushili's last known address – his parent's residence in the plush suburb of Kabulonga. It was unlikely that he would be there but they could not afford to leave any stone unturned. If Paul was to be believed then Amos was in possession of something very precious, something for which he had no qualms about killing anyone who stood in his way. Max wondered what the stolen contraband might be … something small enough to fit in a pocket … jewellry or drugs perhaps? On the face of it the Hinckleys did not seem like the kind who would be engaged in something illegal but then again from the accounting records he had perused through, the farm was not in particularly good shape – he had noticed late payments to suppliers and such. Max had thought carefully, a criminal like Amos would no doubt eventually be seeking a buyer for his stolen goods and the most likely place for such a thing was across the border in Zaire. Zaire was infamous for its trade in stolen contraband. In Max's view it was a free for all, a cesspool of all manner of scoundrels and miscreants. In light of this, Max had sent an urgent message for all border crossings to be on high alert. He had also instructed Jennifer to tell the Chief to send officers out to all of the hotels and motels in Lusaka, there weren't many, in order to check the customer logs. There was a good chance that the *muzungu*, Frits Hubercht, was staying in one of them. As Max manoeuvred his vehicle through the increasingly dense bush, he wondered why this white man, who by all counts seemed to be a close acquaintance of the Hinckleys, would orchestrate a plan to rob them? He sighed, Mutamina's story was hard to believe but sadly he could not say that he was entirely surprised. In his line of work he had seen how money, or the pursuit of it, can drive men to do the most terrible things.

Max and Ronald heard two thumps on the roof. Max pressed his foot against the brake pedal and the car ground to a halt.

"*Ati apo* boss, turn right… just here, turn right here!"

One of the rifle-toting officers barked at Musa. "Are you sure?" Musa gave a tired nod. They had made several wrong turns and back tracked a few times. The two men had struggled to get their bearing right. Max shifted gears and turned the heavy wheel to his right. They moved off the gravel road and into the dense bushes where there seemed to be no discernible track. The two cars behind them ferrying a band of uniformed police officers followed closely. Heads and bodies bobbled up and down as they trundled through the thick foliage.

Several minutes later, Ronald and Max heard another two thumps on the top of their vehicle. Max stopped the car. One of the officers in the back jumped out and began to search the surrounding area. It didn't take long to unearth a set of tire tracks that had been covered by broken branches. Paul and Musa were promptly unshackled and taken from the back of the vehicle to where the officer stood. Max and Ronald followed and were soon facing the two disheveled men.

"Show us exactly where the vehicle was and where you last saw Mushili and the hostage." Ronald said carefully. Paul and Musa recounted everything, pointing to the spots where each man had sat, where Farai the captive had been bound and where they had last seen *ba* Amos. Max stood with his arms akimbo. He surveyed the area – at first sight, there didn't seem to be anything of interest left behind but being the thorough detective that he was, he instructed the officers to search the surrounding bushes for clues.

Moments later an officer called Max and Ronald to come and see what looked like footprints near a clearing. A few snapped twigs provided further credence to the idea that someone, perhaps Mushili, had walked east into the surrounding scrub. Max and Ronald discussed the evidence quietly for a moment standing shoulder to shoulder. "We need to follow the trail and see where it leads." Max said.

Ronald nodded. "Yes boss, I think you're right… but do you think he is still here hiding in the bush – surely, he's long gone?"

Max shook his head. "It's impossible to know. I can see him making a decision either way."

"… and what of the hostage … this Farai chap?"

"There's no telling what the likes of Mushili would do. It's possible he could have taken the hostage with him as a human shield of sorts but I doubt it … it would be inconvenient for him … harder to travel unnoticed."

Ronald rubbed his chin. "So you think that he may have …"

Max shook his head again. "At this point we don't know but the best thing to do would be to follow the trail and keep our eyes open. Mushili is a dangerous man. I also think that we need to fan out in different directions, just in case he's set a decoy … there's no telling what he will do, now he's on the run."

Max turned to the uniformed officers waiting in the wings. He raised his voice. "We need to spread out. If Mushili is anywhere in this bush, we must find him and bring him in. Be warned, this is a very dangerous man … and ruthless when cornered. Each one of you has to be extremely careful as he could be armed and holding a hostage with him. We must make sure we protect ourselves and the life of the hostage … I don't want anyone hurt, you all have families and I want to make sure you return to them in the same way you left them this morning, is that understood?" There was murmuring as the men exchanged nervous glances. Max continued "… *iwe*, you, you and you." Pointing at the men standing furthest away from him. "Go that way." He turned to two other men, "You and you … that way … Detective Siatwinda and I will follow the trail eastwards." Finally, he pointed to the two officers watching over Musa and Paul. "You two … stay here with the vehicles and make sure you keep your eyes on these two." The officers nodded. Max checked his wrist. "… it's thirteen ten now. Let's meet back here no later than seventeen hours. That should give us enough time before it gets dark. Make sure you stick together, don't lose sight of one another!"

29

South to Kariba

The lock to his door needed several shakes before it would open. In his haste, Frits dropped his keys as he entered the room. He cursed before picking them up. He quickly pulled out his duffel bag from where he had left it in the bottom of the wardrobe. Placing it on top of the bed, he rummaged through it until he found what he was looking for – his South African passport. Frits rarely travelled outside of the country, in fact the last time he had travelled was in January of '64, exactly ten months before Zambia's independence. He had travelled to attend his father's burial in Boksberg. When he returned to Zambia, he recalled placing the passport in one of the inside pockets of the duffel bag and put it away. He never thought he would need it again for in October 1964, when Northern Rhodesia became the new sovereign Republic of Zambia, by law, he had automatically become a citizen of the new country. Frits breathed a short sigh of relief, although he had used the bag in the times he had come to see Laura and Henry, he had not bothered to remove the superfluous passport. His thoughts soon returned to the news bulletin he had just heard on the radio while standing in the motel lobby. The police had apprehended two suspects in connection to the Hinckley killings and they were in search of others. The jig was surely up. There wasn't a second to waste, he needed to leave immediately, as long as he was on Zambian soil – he was not safe!

He raced down the corridor. The old man he had noticed before was still working in the flower beds. Passing the lobby, the porter asked if he needed any help with his bag but Frits waved him off and was soon out of the door.

He turned the key to his car and the engine immediately roared into life. Frits reversed out of his parking spot and within seconds was driving through the main gate. A guard in blue uniform stepped out of the red bricked guard house with a notebook in hand waving at him but Frits ignored the man's remonstrations. He peered into his rear view mirror, the guard seemed to be pointing at something ahead but he shrugged it off. In his desperation, Frits had come up with a plan to drive south all the way to the border at Kariba. If he drove fast enough, he could make it into Southern Rhodesia by noon.

He wiped his brow as he drove towards a bend in the road which led from the motel gate. It had all been for naught ... all he had wanted to do was to save his farm and in so doing prevent himself from plummeting into financial ruin but everything had fallen apart. It was as if the entire universe had conspired against him. Why had all his hard work on the farm failed to produce results? Why had Henry suffered a stroke barely a week after they had met in Mukushi? Why had Laura been so intransigent? And for the life of him, he just could not understand why Paul Mutamina and his two-bit thugs had resorted to such gratuitous violence, even when he had explicitly repeated that he did not want anybody to be harmed? He swallowed hard ... It was done now, he could not reverse time – a house that has been burned to the ground cannot be rebuilt from its ashes. Just as Frits turned into the bend in the road he slammed his foot on the break. His car ground to a halt. To his chagrin, there was a fallen tree covering part of the road. A dozen council workers were gathered around working to remove the obstacle. Frits cursed loudly, nothing seemed to be going his way. He squeezed his fingers around the wheel as he watched the men in front of him. Just then, a beige Land Rover appeared on the opposite side of the road – a police vehicle!

The phone on Detective Max Chanda's desk rang three times before Jennifer was able to pick it up. She pinned the receiver to her ear and listened carefully with pen in hand ready to take notes.

"Detective Chanda?"

"No … he is away at the moment … this is his secretary, Jennifer Yumbe … I can take a message sir."

There was noise in the background, the man on the phone seemed a little distracted. "Ah … yes … this is Constable Banda, I'm calling from Kwacha Motel … we've apprehended the suspect … the white man … eh… eh Huba …"

"Hubercht?"

"Yes … we will bring him into Central as soon as we finish searching his room."

30

Appraisal

3:55 p.m.

Inspector General Kalaluka's Office

Independence Avenue, Lusaka

Chief Mbewe straightened the collars on his neatly pressed uniform as he sat waiting outside Inspector General Kalaluka's office. The Inspector had summoned him to his office for a three o'clock meeting. Mbewe had arrived fifteen minutes early and had been waiting for over an hour. During that time he had run and rerun in his mind what he would say to the Inspector. They had made great strides in the Hinckley case: two of the criminals were now in custody and had confessed to the crime. Another had been shot and killed. A fourth suspect was still on the run but they were pursuing him, an ex-convict by the name of Amos Mushili. There was also cause to believe that he had a captive with him but that was yet to be confirmed. Finally, they had also apprehended a person of interest in the case – a white man, a Boer, who was alleged to have orchestrated the whole thing. Chief Mbewe was feeling rather satisfied with how things had gone so far – Detective Maxwell Chanda had performed well.

The Chief watched as Inspector Kalaluka's young secretary tapped away at her typewriter - fast and purposefully. Every few minutes she would lift her head and he would shift his gaze. She reminded him of his wife in her younger days – petite with delicate features. After several more minutes of waiting, the door to the Inspector's office opened. Chief Mbewe instinctively took to his feet and straightened his uniform. To his surprise Peter James, the tall white man from the British Embassy who had come to his office a few days earlier, stepped out of the office. The two men looked at each other, a smirk lingering on Peter's face. "Chief *Mbe-wee*" he said with a nod of his head. Mbewe greeted him, they locked eyes for an awkward moment before Peter James made his way across the foyer and out the door to the outside. What was he doing here? What business did he have with the Inspector General of Police? This could not be good.

"He will see you now," the secretary said softly.

The Inspector sat silently as Chief Mbewe went through his rehearsed appraisal of the Hinckley case. When he was done Inspector Kalaluka shifted in his seat, a frown on his face. "Was it you who ordered the search of Justice Mushili's residence in Kabulonga?"

Mbewe felt a chill in the air. He cleared his throat. "Sir, we received reliable intelligence ..."

"I see nothing intelligent about raiding the house of a retired Chief Justice ... and the bumbling idiots even had the gumption to enter the room of Mama Mushili while she was undressed!"

Mbewe felt hot around the collar, this was not at all how he had expected things to turn out. "...sir ... I ... I can explain sir ..."

The Inspector waved his hand. "You say you have apprehended suspects that have hitherto confessed to crime, not so?"

"Ye... yes sir"

"And this *muzungu*, the Boer, how is he implicated in this whole thing?"

Chief Mbewe was relieved to be talking about the facts of the case again. "Well sir, we understand ... well ... the two other suspects in custody have revealed that the whole thing was planned and orchestrated by the white man. He was a close friend to the slain couple."

The Inspector frowned. "And what was his motive, are you sure these thugs are not just making up stories to save themselves?"

Mbewe continued. "We are led to believe that there was some

contraband hidden in a safe that the Boer wanted."

"Contraband? What exactly are you referring to?"

Mbewe scratched the back of his neck. "We're not sure yet, sir. The white man is not talking, he's denying everything sir, but we are working on him ... he will talk sir."

Inspector Kalaluka locked his fingers in front of his face and pondered the information for a moment. Finally, he straightened his back in his chair. "I want you to wrap up this case right now. We have apprehended suspects who have confessed to the crime. This connection to the *muzungu* sounds fanciful to me, these two bit criminals are trying to save their skins by making up stories. I see no reason at all to entertain these machinations. I'm scheduled to brief State House this evening at nineteen hours and I must give a positive account on this case. Following that, there is to be a press briefing first thing tomorrow morning." He stared directly at Chief Mbewe. "Mbewe, this cannot loom over the Heads of Government summit ... I don't need to remind you about the political sensitivity of this case, do I?"

"No ... no sir."

"Good. I'm glad that we understand each other."

Chief Mbewe nodded his head. "Yes sir." He knew not to argue with his superior officer.

31

Hot on the Trail

Three officers combed through the forest in a straight line a few yards apart. They kept each other in view as they moved quietly through the bush. Leaves and twigs crackled underfoot as they steadily progressed. Each man's heart was doing laps for they had all heard the rumours about Amos Kapambwe Mushili: a ruthless killer who possessed supernatural powers. There was talk of how he had killed a woman and then brutally attacked a fellow inmate in prison. Many said that Amos had caused the untimely deaths of the children of prison guards who had dared to stand in his way. The men had whispered among themselves but were fearful of voicing their apprehensions in front of their superiors. As the men walked on they could hear the sound of birds chirping high in the trees and the occasional fluttering of wings in amongst the branches. Approximately two hours had elapsed since they had embarked on their search, they would soon need to start heading back to their rendezvous point to make it before dark. There was still no sign of Mushili nor of Farai Muguru, the captive.

"Ksssss!" Hissed one of the men suddenly. They all stopped and exchanged nervous glances. Each man crouched down to his haunches beneath the bushes. One of the officers pointed at something ahead as he craned his neck to peer through the scrub. There was something hidden in the foliage several yards ahead of them. Signalling to one another they moved slowly in a manner as if to encircle whatever it was that was lurking ahead of them. Hearts pounding, mouths dry, they raised their rifles.

Max and Ronald journeyed quietly through the dense brush. Max panned the area ahead of him, every direction looked the same; it would be easy to get lost. He hoped that his men had heeded his words to stick together. They soon reached a tall tree with a thick trunk that dwarfed the surrounding vegetation. Ronald made his way to the base of the tree and planted his foot inside a large cleavage in its trunk. "I think we're quite near the main road," Ronald said as he pulled himself up by the arms and climbed nimbly up into the branches; Max admired his dexterity briefly remembering the days when he too had taken pleasure in climbing trees. Ronald looked into the distance, "I can't see the road but there's a small village ... one ... maybe two kilometres away!" Max glanced down at his watch. They still had time. They could make it there and back to their rendezvous point before dark.

The three officers waited with baited breath, their rifles held at the ready and their eyes fixed ahead. They inched forward, careful not to make a sound. Then, through the leaves, they saw him – a man hiding in the bushes!

※

Max and Ronald watched as a shirtless little boy raced towards a cluster of mud huts several metres away. The boy's threadbare shorts exposed his small buttocks as he disappeared from view. The two detectives stood at a clearing as they waited for him to return. It was a small rural setting, there could not be more than a handful of people living here, most likely subsistence farmers who lived off the land. Ronald turned to Maxwell. "Boss, do you really think he'd hide in such a place?"

Max shook his head. "Unlikely, it's far enough away from the main road but he would not feel safe here, it's a tiny village and so it'd be impossible to be anonymous ... but let's see if someone saw or heard something in the surrounding area."

The little boy appeared again in the distance with a buxom woman trailing in his wake. When she was upon them, they exchanged greetings, she clapped her hands gently and introduced herself as *bana* Sikazwe. Her demeanour was of one who was accustomed to being called to help for one thing or another. They asked her if she knew of any strangers or visitors staying in the village or anyone who may have passed through in the past day or so. She nodded immediately. Max and Ronald exchanged glances. Max looked at her closely, she had a round face with two sets of tribal markings at her temples. The woman went on to describe how she had been called to attend to a man, a Rhodesian by the name of Farai Muguru, who had been found lying in the bushes by a group of girls who were on their way back from drawing water. She said that she was a midwife, the only one in the village, and hence was frequently called upon whenever anyone was hurt or sick, she seemed proud of this fact. They asked her to describe him and if the man was still in the village, to which *bana* Sikazwe shook her head. He had been taken to the clinic in town. She then described him as young, probably in his thirties, medium build. The man had appeared disheveled, covered in dirt, cuts and bruises, he was very ill. It was as if he had been chased by something, an animal perhaps? He did not have a temperature but he was very weak and, she had given him some water but, in the abundance of caution, she had instructed two young men to take him to the nearest clinic in town. She was quick to add that if the man had been brought to her sooner, she might have been able to tend to him with her traditional herbs but he seemed past that point.

Maxwell asked if there was another person with him. She said there was no one else with him. Max then asked to talk to the girls who had found him as well as to the young men who had taken him to the clinic. In a short time, a group of teenage girls were able to describe to Max and Ronald what they had seen and show them where they had noticed the man in the bushes. Again, like *bana* Sikazwe, they said they had not seen anyone else with him.

Finally, the two men who had taken Farai to the clinic were called to speak with the two detectives. They described how they had carried him to the main road a few kilometres away and hitched a ride into Kapiri. They had made sure to leave the man in the care of the nurses at the clinic before returning. They said that after examining him, the nurse had told them that he would be fine. She had surmised that he was probably suffering from exhaustion or low sugar levels. She had placed him on a drip and said that with some rest, he would recover. With the nurse's assurance, they had left him to rest and returned to the village. Max noted down these details into his notepad. They would have to check out the clinic as soon as they returned to Kapiri. It was imperative to track down Farai for he would have important details that could prove vital in catching Amos Mushili. For now Max was able to breathe a sigh of relief, they still had work to do but he was comforted in the knowledge that the hostage that Mushili and his thugs had taken was unharmed.

The three officers signalled silently to each other, they would pounce at the count of three. It would take all three of them to face the ignoble Amos Kapambwe Mushili. Each man steeled himself. One … two … three…

Max and Ronald felt an air of jubilation in the camp as soon as they returned to the rendezvous point. "*Natumuusanga*! We've found him, *sah*!" One of the officers said as he rose to his feet. The two detectives exchanged glances.

"You've captured Mushili?" Ronald asked expectantly.

One of the officers standing several feet away spoke up. "No *sah* … it's the hostage … Farai Muguru, we found him and brought him back safely."

Max and Ronald looked at each other again. Maxwell took a step forward. "Are you sure? … Take me to him."

Amos Mushili had executed his plan to perfection. His gamble had paid off. He knew the heat was on and that the police would be searching every nook and cranny for them. Trying to evade the authorities as a group would have been a fool's wager. He made the decision to take the precious uncut stones and save himself.

In the hours following their attack on Hinckley Farm, Amos had made sure to take Farai Muguru's identification papers and shoved them into his pocket as they stuffed their captive into the boot of the car. He would later scratch Farai's picture on the papers so that it appeared faded and difficult to make out. Driving through the night, Amos had conjured his plan. He would wait until they had found a place to hide out for some time. He would then spike their food with the date-rape drug he had planned to use on the dogs at the farm. He was sure that if he used the right amount it would knock the men out cold and give him the opportunity to make his escape. There was no such thing as loyalty among thieves.

Amos knew that they were no more than ten kilometres west of the main road and that he would have to make his way eastwards through the bush. He had stumbled upon a small village and hidden in the scrub. He needed a way to evade the police at the checkpoints leading into the town and what better way than to pose as an ailing patient in desperate need of medical attention? So Amos smeared himself with dirt, covering himself with cuts and bruises, the scar on his left cheek masked in clay. Then he lay himself down a few feet from a well-trodden footpath and waited.

Amos had been patient, he had allowed the two young men to carry him all the way to the clinic in Kapiri. All the while the men had not known what danger they had put themselves in for Amos was willing and able to use deadly force if the need arose in order to evade being captured.

6:22 p.m.

Tambalale Clinic, Kapiri Mposhi

The nurse shook her head and gave a wry smile. "Look around you detective … we see hundreds of patients every day, we open from eight in the morning and close at eighteen thirty, there are usually only two of us here." Max empathised with her, he knew all too well what it was like to work in an overburdened government institution with little help. He nodded.

"I understand but please think hard and try your best to remember. Did he say anything, anything at all about where he was going?"

The nurse thought for a moment but was soon distracted by the noise of an infant crying behind her. She shook her head. "I'm sorry detective, I cannot recall him saying anything about where he was going. All I know is that as soon as he felt better, he left ... to where, I don't know."

DAY 5

Tuesday, July 25th 1979

32

A Peace-Loving Nation

6:44 a.m.

British Foreign Office, King Charles Street, Westminster, London

Secretary David Owen paced the polished floor behind his desk. The Queen traveling to open a Commonwealth meeting was not supposed to cause him sleepless nights. He needed to issue a security briefing about her impending trip in two hours' time and if he did not get any good news from Zambia, he would be compelled to recommend that her majesty's travel plans be shelved. Government could ill afford the bad press the Hinckley murders were generating but he could only imagine the political furor cancelling the trip would generate. Just then, the telephone rang, He picked it up and waited for the switchboard to connect the call.

"Peter? … Any good news for me?" He listened intently for a moment. He breathed a sigh of relief. "I'm glad to hear it. That's certainly good news, well done." He said. He listened again as his in-country attaché briefed him some more. Finally, he nodded his head. "Good, very good. I'm happy to hear that it's all been settled." He then hung up the telephone.

✳

9:12 a.m.
Great North Road, city limits, Lusaka

Amos Mushili had slipped through their fingers. Max knew that Mushili could be anywhere in the country even have made it across the border. It was now a waiting game and in cases like this it often took a stroke of good fortune to catch the criminal – a diligent border officer noticing something, a citizen observing something unusual and reporting it to the authorities or even a random traffic stop yielding dividends. Max had not lost hope of catching Mushili, but he knew it would take time, perhaps more time than his boss was willing to give him. Max and Ronald had decided to head back to Lusaka in the early hours of Tuesday morning. Max was keen to interrogate the *muzungu*, Frits Hubercht, who was now being held in remand at Lusaka Central Police Station.

It was a little after nine o'clock in the morning when they approached the city limits of Lusaka. Max turned on his car radio. It took several seconds to catch the signal then he heard the radio announcer say that there was a live press briefing about to commence outside the office of the Inspector General of Police.

9:15 a.m.
Press Briefing outside Inspector General Kalaluka's Office
Independence Avenue, Lusaka

There was a furious spate of flashing cameras as Inspector General Kalaluka stepped behind a table that had been set on the south lawn of his office building and covered by a tablecloth in the colours of the national flag. The inspector took his seat behind a set of microphones which covered part of his face. The murmur of reporters was mixed with the mechanical clicking and wheezing of cameras and recording equipment. Inspector Kalaluka waited for a signal from his press aide.

The Inspector cleared his throat into to the microphones. "Good … good morning distinguished ladies and gentlemen, honourable ministers, members of the diplomatic corps, members of the press, civil servants and my fellow citizens." His numerous medals pinned across his chest glistened in the sunlight. He peered down at his typed sheet of paper. "I'd like to thank all of you for attending this briefing and to thank all of you that are listening through your radios." He cleared his throat again. "Yesterday evening I was able to brief his Excellency the President, Dr Kenneth David Kaunda about some key developments in a very high-profile police investigation that has captured the attention of this nation and beyond." He looked up into the cameras as they clicked in rapid unison. "My fellow countrymen and women, a few days ago we lost two renowned citizens of our great and young nation – Mr and Mrs Henry and Laura Hinckley through an act of senseless violence. Indeed our nation lost two of our heroes in the freedom struggle." He paused to let the gravity of the loss sink in. "As I'm sure you have read in the media, the Hinckleys fell victim at their *home*," he paused for emphasis, "by a gang of ruthless thugs." He paused again. "My fellow citizens, such a violent crime is alien to us for we are a peace-loving people and our president, His Excellency Kaunda, has always preached Humanism and love ... love for one another as citizens of this great nation. We must never allow such criminal behaviour to go unpunished and so with the full support of our president, we launched a concerted investigation to bring to justice all who perpetrated this heinous crime" Inspector General Kalaluka shuffled his papers. "Fellow citizens, having received the permission of his Excellency Kenneth David Kaunda, I would like to inform you that we have succeeded in this mission. *All* the perpetrators of this crime have been apprehended." He raised a finger in triumph. "*All* the perpetrators have been detained and signed confessions secured." The mumbling of the gathering grew louder and the cameras flashed. "I would like to inform the country and indeed the world that this beautiful country of ours, Zambia, will never condone violence ... we are a peace-loving people and we welcome all people regardless of race, colour or creed. We welcome all of you out there to come and visit our lovely, peaceful nation."

He held his sheets of paper between his fingers and looked up with a proud smile.

"A formal police statement will be issued by the end of the day with the names of all the criminals and they will swiftly be taken to answer for their crimes in our judicial system. May God almighty bless all of you and your families and our great nation." The cameras flashed relentlessly as he stood up and stepped away from the microphones. Soon the Inspector disappeared into the office building, armed policemen shielding the door.

33

The Right Thing to Do

Maxwell Chanda was beside himself. Usually a man of unshakable temperament, he found it difficult to contain his anger. "Sir, this flies in the face of everything we hold true as officers of the law … we … we have an oath to fulfil … an oath to serve and protect …"

Chief Mbewe raised his palm. He had never seen his best detective this animated before. "Chanda… Chanda … I'm aware of the oath we took as officers … but this thing is big …it's bigger than you or I, do you understand what I'm saying?"

Max breathed heavily. He squeezed his right fist for a moment before unclenching it in an attempt to calm himself. "Sir, there is a man out there …" He pointed to the window "… there's a dangerous criminal out there roaming the streets … sir, we cannot pretend that all is well. Men like Mushili don't just stop committing crimes, he will do it again if we don't catch him … I can guarantee you that he will kill again and if he does, that blood will be on our hands!"

Chief Mbewe attempted to reason with Max. "Listen to me Chanda, I'm not saying that we just forget about him, I share your concern, believe me I do. All I'm saying is that we put it on hold for a little while, just until this whole thing with the Commonwealth summit and the Queen of England is behind us. You can still look into one or two things quietly for now… you know … but just don't make any waves until this thing blows over. There's just too much politics surrounding it, that's all."

Max was unimpressed. "But sir, you know as well as I do that the longer we wait, the colder the trail gets, we might never be able to catch him."

Mbewe sighed. He hunched over his desk in resignation. He began to speak slowly. "Chanda, listen to me, eh … trust me on this one, this thing is too hot, there are foreign governments involved … people at the highest levels, people who can cause us problems at the snap of a finger. Chanda, you have a wife and children …" The Chief paused before correcting himself. "… a child." Max lowered his eyes. "Chanda, think about them before you do anything rash… don't let your stubbornness destroy their lives and everything that you've built in your long career. Sometimes it's best to do what we are told even though we may not like it or necessarily agree with it, it's part and parcel of being a team player." He looked up at Max who was now sitting in silent contemplation. "Detective Chanda, can I count on you to be a team player?"

It just wasn't right and Maxwell knew it but he thought about his family at home, his wife and son and how he had barely spent time with them in over a week. He recalled where he had left things with Mavis before he left for Kapiri, how she had wanted him to open up to her and how he had failed in his duty to be emotionally present for her following the death of their daughter Lindiwe. He knew he had abrogated his responsibilities as a husband and father and it pained him every time he thought about it. Max sighed heavily before lifting his head slowly. "I would like to question the white man…"

34

The Art of Interrogation

An uncomfortable silence hung in the room as if a death had just been announced. Even the perennial sound of Jennifer tapping on her typewriter had ceased. Max sank into his chair, his eyes fixed to a spot on top of his desk. It was Ronald Siatwinda who broke the stillness. "…but what about Mushili? … I mean we can't just let him get away with it … . Surely …"

Max shook his head disconsolately. "There's political involvement at the highest levels … it's a direct order from the Chief … and you heard the Inspector General's public briefing this morning."

"… yes Boss, but … but we can't just let him get away … he's a dangerous criminal … and … and whatever happened to seeking justice?" Ronald sounded exasperated. Jennifer glanced at him, a rare expression of admiration entering her face – maybe she had misjudged him after all, perhaps he was not as self-serving and egotistical as she had thought. Max parted his lips as if to speak but decided against it. There was no point in arguing the matter, powerful people above him had made a decision based on political expediency not on what was the right thing to do. They had latched onto the simplest narrative, one which they felt would appease the public and foreign governments: "Three criminals had invaded the Hinckley Farm and slain Mr and Mrs Hinckley in their sleep. The men had been subsequently pursued by the Zambian authorities. One of the men was shot and killed while the other two had been apprehended and had confessed to the crime". In this report which had now been formally released to the press, there was no Frits Hubercht and no Amos Mushili. The police had formally charged Paul and Musa for the crime and would soon be releasing Frits from police custody. In Max's eyes it was nothing short of a travesty of justice and he wanted no part of it. He understood, however that he was now on his own. In order to catch Mushili he would have to do it alone without the backing of his Chief nor the department and he was running out of time. He also acknowledged the salient fact that he would be risking it all – his career, his family and quite possibly his life.

✳

Max sat at his desk that afternoon reading through his case notes. He had also obtained the transcript of the interrogation that the arresting officers had conducted on the white man, Frits Hubercht. Frits was still in remand but was slated to be released the next morning. He knew that he would need to interrogate Frits for himself but under the current circumstances he would have to do it discretely. In addition, his years of experience had taught him that preparation is the cornerstone of a successful interrogation. He recalled the mantra of his favourite lecturer in the academy, a retired British officer by the name of Lloyd Jones, who used to say: *"The goal of a good investigator is not to know all the answers but to understand the questions."*

Max waited until Ronald and Jennifer had left for the day and much of the station had emptied. Then he made his way downstairs. There were two junior officers, one male the other female, manning the holding cells. They stopped their conversation and took to their feet in salute as he stood in front of them. Max greeted them, he recognised their faces but couldn't recall their names.

"I need to speak with a suspect, the white man, can you bring him out to the interrogation room?" He asked. The two officers glanced at each other. It was unusual for a senior level officer to come down and specifically request that a suspect be released into his charge, they typically sent their underlings to do it. "I need to clear up some case notes, he will be returned shortly." Max added.

❋

Max had many questions for Frits but so little time in which to get answers. He had read from the transcripts that Frits had thus far been uncooperative – unsurprisingly, he had denied any involvement in the Hinckley killings. He had insisted that Laura and Henry were his closest friends and he had no reason to want them dead – the whole notion was preposterous and hurtful. But Max did not believe him, many things just did not add up. For instance, Max and Ronald had interrogated Musa and Paul and from his estimation the two men were incapable of orchestrating such a high stakes and bloody farm invasion. They lacked the intellect, the means and the daring to do it by themselves. Of course there was the dead suspect, Mambwe, but he was Musa's equal and he too would not have had the skills and gumption to lead the charge. Amos was most certainly a central figure in this case and even Farai, the Rhodesian hostage who they had taken, corroborated this observation. Frits' denials also rang hollow because how else would Paul have known him? It was unlikely that a young black ex-convict would suddenly just strike up a friendship with a white man. No, there had to be more to the story. So far all of Paul's accounts of dates and encounters checked out to be accurate. Another question looming in Max's head was why Frits had called the police station and asked to speak to the detective in charge of the investigation. Was it a ploy to divert any suspicion from him? – But that seemed foolish, or was there something else that he wanted? Max was also desperate to know exactly what was in the Hinckley safe and why Amos had exhibited such brutality in getting it?

Getting a suspect to divulge information about themselves that might help in solving a case is nothing short of an art. Everything is deliberate and nothing should be left to chance. Maxwell knew that if he was to get answers out of Frits, he would have to be at his best.

Maxwell checked his wrist for the third time, it was now exactly forty two minutes since a junior officer had placed Frits inside the interrogation room. **Lesson #1**: Keep the suspect waiting alone indefinitely in an empty room, it serves to unnerve him, making his imagination run wild.

174

The door opened suddenly with a creak at the hinges as Max entered the tiny room. Frits was a large man, he had an ominous presence and his sweaty musk filled the room. Frits looked dishevelled sitting on the cement floor with his wrists and ankles shackled. Max held the door ajar and called for an officer to unshackle the suspect. **Lesson #2:** Show empathy, it helps build trust. Once Frits was unshackled, Max asked to be left alone with him. The officer seemed hesitant but Max insisted. "Please, take a seat." Max pointed to an empty wooden chair. The two men took their positions across from each other with nothing but an empty table and a manila folder stuffed with papers which Max had lain on top of it. They sat silently for a moment, a battle of wills already waged. Max spoke first. "I understand you asked to see me…" Frits flexed his wrists, the shackles had left bruises on his skin. His eyes met Max's but he remained mum. "My name is Maxwell Chanda … Detective Maxwell Chanda. I head the special crimes unit here at Central … you left word for me two days ago that you wanted to speak with me. What was it that you wanted to talk to me about?"

Frits shifted in his seat before scratching his jaw. Max watched his every movement with a keen eye. **Lesson #3:** Pay close attention to non-verbal cues, ninety percent of all communication is non-verbal. "Laura and Henry were close friends of mine … they'd just been killed on their farm … I needed to talk to the investigator in charge … to see how I could help with the investigation."

Max nodded. "I see … and how did you learn of … how did you hear about what happened at Hinckley Farm?"

"In the newspaper … like everyone else."

"Yes, it was big news all across the country. You live in Mukushi … you have a farm there?" Max continued.

Frits nodded. "Yes"

"How long have you lived there?"

"Since … just over six years …" Frits looked upwards to his right as he answered the question. Max took note. Scientific study has it that when a suspect is remembering something, their eyes shift upwards to the right.

"And how long have you known the Hinckleys?"

Frits thought for a moment. His eyes again shifting upwards to the right. "Hey ... I've known Henry since ... hey ... I don't know ... I've known him for at least twenty ... twenty-five years ... Laura a little less than that, but a long time."

"And since you've known them, has there been any trouble? Any cause for anyone to wish them ill or to harm them?"

Frits shook his head. His eyes shifted to his left – a cognitive reflex, a suspect thinking about something typically shifts their eyes upwards to the left. "I don't know of ..." At this point Max pulled out a pen and a ring-bound notepad from his pocket and laid it on top of the table. The action interrupted Frits's train of thought.

"Please continue ..."

Frits went on to state that he knew of nothing or anyone who would wish the Hinckley's harm, they were good, kind people who treated everyone well even the workers on their farm. Max bristled inside but he did not show it. He knew many *muzungus* like Frits and how they saw black Africans. Frits spoke as if treating one's black employees humanely was something to be heralded as somehow benevolent – when would they learn that this was Africa, a black man's land!

Max scribbled some notes into his notepad. "Tell me about Henry Hinckley, what was he like? ... I understand he was very sick towards the end of his life ... suffered a stroke." Frits gladly went on to describe a dear friend with whom he had spent much of his younger days working in the mineral prospecting industry. **Lesson #4**: Develop a rapport, the suspect drops his guard and begins to reveal details that might prove useful. Maxwell then asked his suspect to talk about Laura and Hinckley Farm as well as when he had last seen the Hinckleys.

Maxwell continued to take notes, he mostly listened and nodded with the occasional question to encourage Frits to continue or to elaborate at key points. Max didn't know how much Frits knew concerning the current atmosphere surrounding the case. Although all suspects held in remand were isolated from the media, it was impossible to know if anything had filtered through to them. He did not know if Frits knew of his impending release the following day and that the police were officially closing the investigation altogether. Biding his time, Max allowed Frits to continue talking.

"Paul Mutamina, Amos Mushili, do any of these names ring a bell?" Max asked suddenly. **Lesson #5:** Switch the conversation without warning, it unsettles the suspect. Frits paused, for a fleeting moment his eyes shifted upwards to the left. He shook his head.

"No."

Max lifted the manila folder from the table and began to flick through it. Frits watched him closely. "Are you aware of Ifundo Milling Company?" Frits hesitated. "It's in Kafue district, not too far from Hinckley Farm … records show they supply many farms in that area with livestock feed, including Hinckley Farm."

"Ah yes …I just couldn't remember the name." His hand moved to his chin.

Max continued calmly. "Have you ever visited the establishment at all?"

Frits' eyes shifted upwards to the left. "Hey … I may have … I'm not sure … maybe."

"Hmmm" Max shuffled through papers in his folder. "One of the suspects that we apprehended in the Hinckley case claims to have made your acquaintance at Ifundo Milling Company … a man by the name of Paul Mutamina. There are confirmed eye witnesses to it." Max had no such witnesses.

Frits shook his head. "No … I … no that name doesn't ring a bell."

Max searched his folder again, right then left and right again. He stopped and then looked up at Frits. "Tell me Mr. Hubercht, how long have you been in financial trouble?" **Lesson #6:** The confrontation, at an appropriate point the interrogator must go in for the kill using the facts – real or perceived. Frits shifted uncomfortably in his seat, the room suddenly feeling smaller than before. He moved his mouth but did not utter. Max had no definitive evidence that Frits was in financial trouble but he had added two and two together.

Most murders boiled down to either crimes of passion or greed, this certainly was not a crime of passion. Something of intrinsic value had been taken from the Hinckley's safe and if Frits, a close friend, was involved then a likely motivation was that he desperately needed money and was prepared to steal from them. Had he enough time, Max would have dug into Frits' past to find out whether or not he had any large debts that he was failing to pay. There was also the small fact of where the police had apprehended Frits, at Kwacha Motel – that was not the kind of place where a white man with means would ordinarily stay.

Frits lips quivered. Max had touched a nerve. "I … I there's money owed …I've a bank loan on the farm … yes … which I'm paying off…"

Max looked at him squarely. He imagined Frits to be a man who had intimidated many with his size but here in this forum it was clear where the balance of power lay and it was not with him. "Mr Hubercht, I urge you to speak plainly. I assure you that it will be better for you if you tell me the whole truth. What exactly was your involvement in what happened that night at the Hinckley Farm?"

35

Homecoming

11:02 p.m.

Chilenje, Lusaka

The Lusaka city streets were empty by the time Max left the station. He had succeeded in getting what he needed from Frits Hubercht, a written statement detailing his involvement in the Hinckley killings. He recalled how Frits had crumbled into a ball of emotions as he took to describing how his ill-advised intentions to save his farm had cascaded into a catalogue of events that were beyond his control. He had sworn through tears that he had never meant for anyone to be hurt, he said the deaths of Laura and Henry would haunt him for the rest of his life and pleaded for compassion. Max rubbed the back of his neck, with everything going on he was exhausted and had not been home since arriving earlier in the day. He turned a corner into a narrow dusty street, a broken street lamp marking the entry into Chilenje, his modest neighbourhood. He wished he could afford to live in one of the wealthier areas like Kabulonga or Roma but that was not possible on a police detective's salary. He thought about his family, Mavis and his son Chipasha, they deserved more, in a way he understood what drove men to make bad decisions in a bid to provide for their families. Much as he wished to better his lot in life, he would never resort to crime, it took a cold heart and, or desperation to organise a band of thieves to rob your closest friends. He imagined a big man like Frits, used to getting his own way, accustomed to a sense of superiority, suddenly bankrupt and diminished. No better than the blacks he despised. Was it enough to make him resort to desperate measures, to lose whatever sense of morality he possessed?

The AM signal on his radio fluttered as he drove past a telephone pole. He could see lights behind curtains in some of the homes on either side of the road – night owls like him who found it hard to sleep. Max was satisfied that he had managed to get a comprehensive account from Frits – a signed admission of guilt. However, he knew that he would have to tread carefully with the information as it directly contradicted the official narrative of the police force. That was a fight for another day. He would present the statement to Chief Mbewe in the morning, he would be displeased but even he could not ignore it, he would not be able to allow Frits to be released. As a compromise, Max would suggest that the whole matter be kept from the press until after the Commonwealth summit. He arrived at the rusted gate to his house, a shoulder high wire fence surrounding his small yard. The lights in his house were turned off except for the two security lamps above the verandah. He got out of his car and opened the gate.

Mavis opened the door from inside the house as soon as he stepped onto the verandah, car keys in one hand and his small travel bag in the other. A doek over her head, a *chitenge* wrapped around her and knotted under her shoulder, Mavis spoke softly. "*Mwabweleni bashi* Chipasha." A sense of guilt tightened around Max's throat. He remembered how they had left things, the words unsaid that threatened to overwhelm them. They hadn't spoken for almost two days but the tension was still there, ever present and difficult to ignore like a stone in one's shoe.

"I'm sorry to wake you." He said. Her eyes looked everywhere but at him. She folded her arms as if to ward off the cold.

"*Ingileni na bwila*, it's late. I'll prepare something for you to eat." She said as she stepped back into the house.

Maxwell stepped out of the shower and dried himself with a towel. The water had been lukewarm on account of the geyser having been turned off to save electricity. His thoughts drifted to Amos Mushili and how he still had no clue as to where to find him. In his confession, Frits had insisted he did not know Amos, he was a man who Paul Mutamina had solicited to help with the mission of retrieving the contraband, a handful of uncut emeralds, from the Hinckley's safe. Max wiped down the last droplets of moisture on his arms and legs and stood in front of the bathroom mirror. Streams of blood for a fistful of gemstones.

He found three covered plates set on a tray on the kitchen table. A welcoming aroma of a home cooked meal hung in the air – fresh *nshima*, dried fish and *kalembula*. Mavis had her back turned to him while she washed a set of dishes in the sink. Max stood in the doorway and took it all in for a moment. How fortunate he was to have *this* home and *this* woman in *this* life. She had shown him love despite the depth of pain that only a mother can feel after the loss of a child. Indeed she had loved him even when he had failed to show her love and affection. Max crossed the threshold into the kitchen, Mavis had not heard him on account of the running faucet. She flinched, startled by his touch and then froze, the muscles in her back growing taut as he gently circled his arms around her from behind. He breathed on the back of her shoulder. "I … I'm sorry." He said softly. "I'm so sorry."

The Arrival
Thursday, July 28th 1979

36

KK - Queenie!

10:23 a.m.

Airport Road, Lusaka

School children in grey safari uniforms lined along the banks of Airport Road. Their spit polished shoes glistened in the bright sunlight, each child with their white socks drawn to their knees. The lines stretched into the distance as far as the eye could see. There was an electric buzz in the air as most people had only ever seen the Queen of England in newspaper pictures. The arrival of a foreign head of state was always met with fanfare but this one was special, it had a different feel to it … she wasn't just a leader of a nation, she was royalty!

The children clapped and waved their hands, broad smiles of anticipation as a motorcade appeared on the horizon. At best, most people would probably only get a glimpse of her but that did little to abet the excitement. Traditional drums thundered in rhythmic beats as the *vinyau* men in her masks and with their bodies doused in paint danced feverishly. Women and men sang songs they had been rehearsing for weeks at the tops of their voices. The moment had arrived.

"*Bafika! Bafika! Bafika!*" Came the shouts from yonder. A string of roaring motorcycles was the first to pass by. Uniformed men wearing helmets marshalled there mechanical horses with the pomp that the occasion deserved, their heads aloft and shoulders erect like preening peacocks. Then a convoy of identical black Mercedes Benz sedans followed. Soldiers on heightened alert fixed their eyes on the jubilant crowd.

Finally they saw it, the President Kenneth Kaunda's signature white handkerchief waiving from a window of a black Rolls Royce. The vehicle gleamed impeccably in the sun. The crowd went into a frenzy. They screamed at the tops of their lungs, all the while straining their eyes to see through the windows of the car. Perched on the passenger's seat to the left of the president was a rather plain middle-aged white lady in a yellow gown and a matching floral hat.

"*Ba Queenie abo! Ba Queenie!*" And then the chants began. "*KK – Queenie! KK – Queenie! KK – Queenie!*"

The Queen of England lifted an experienced gloved hand and waved to the adoring crowd.

❉

Barely three kilometres away from the pomp and circumstance of Queen Elizabeth's arrival, Maxwell Chanda sat alone in his office. Ronald had been swept by the euphoria that had overtaken the country and was somewhere in amongst the throngs of people welcoming the British Monarch. Jennifer Yumbe had asked for a couple of days leave to attend to personal family matters on the Copperbelt. Max had been quick to oblige her request considering that she had worked long hours during the past week as they investigated the Hinckley case.

Max leaned back into his chair and stared at the room in front of him. Plastic folders on shelves, papers piled on top of each other, they certainly needed to do some re-arranging but there never seemed to be enough time. He pressed the tips of his fingers together, there was still no sign nor word of Mushili. It was as if he had disappeared into thin air, vanished from the face of the earth. Max was concerned about where he was and what he might do next, there was no telling what a dangerous man like that would do. Following Frits' admission, Max had since sought the advice of gemstone dealers in the city on how one might attempt to find a buyer for a stash of illegal stones. Many had said that the best way would be to find a foreign buyer and that meant moving across the border with the most likely destination being Zaire. Max was crestfallen, had they missed their opportunity to catch Mushili had it not been for the political influence in the case? He remembered the tall lanky white man that had sat in the Chief's office a week ago bearing a glib expression on his face. He recalled how it had rankled him. Had he interfered in the Hinckley case, played some role in the Chief or indeed the Inspector General's decision making? It was impossible to know for sure. In Max's estimation it was conceivable that had it not been for the Commonwealth summit, they may perhaps have been able to locate Amos Mushili. Keeping the public's attention during the first few days of a manhunt could not be overstated, every day the suspect remained at large, the harder it was to capture him. Just then, the telephone on his desk rang.

"Hello, Detective Chanda speaking."

"Hello *sah* … there was an incident last night *sah* … you need to come out …"

37

Subterfuge

9:48 p.m.

Night before Queen Elizabeth's arrival

Woodlands, Lusaka

Peter James nodded as he read through the papers in his hands. "Yes …" he said. "Yes, this … this is exactly what I was after." He looked up and smiled, satisfaction and relief in equal measure. "Where are my manners, would you care for a drink?"

"Why of course, I can never say no to that. I'll have whatever brand of whisky you have." Amos said as he stretched himself out on Peter's sofa.

"You're an easy man to please." Peter said as he turned towards the wooden cabinet behind him. He folded the thin sheets of paper into a square and placed them into his shirt pocket. He considered Mushili's brash familiarity to be uncouth but he masked his mild irritation in a manner typical of a British gentleman. He placed two empty glasses onto a silver tray and began to pour a golden beverage into them. When he was done, he turned and slowly traversed the room. The walls were festooned with animal busts, trophies from his hunting expeditions. He handed a glass to Mushili before taking a seat in the armchair facing him.

Mushili held his glass up for a toast. "Here's to escaping in one piece, I went through hell to get you that little pamphlet." Peter raised his glass, "To you" he said. The two men drank from their glasses. Amos swirled his glass before taking another mouthful. "Ah! … trust the stuffy British to have the finest shit." He said looking down at his drink. Peter leant into his chair before crossing his legs. "So what's so important about that list of names anyway? … I mean why did you want it so badly?"

Peter took a sip from his glass again. "This list of names and addresses…" he said tapping at his pocket. "… is more valuable than the fistful of uncut emeralds that you took from the Hinckley's safe."

Mushili cackled. "Is that right? Well … if you say so … I guess to each his own." Peter eyed Amos from above his glass. He was certainly a flawed character and he had had his reservations about using him but sometimes in his line of work the end justified the means. Peter James thought back to everything that had transpired over the past year and the decisions he had been forced to make, such was the life of a British intelligence officer. He had first met Amos on one evening in early 1974 at the poolside of Pamodzi Hotel. A mutual friend had introduced Amos as the son of Judge Mushili who at that time was a shoe-in to become Chief Justice of the country. Ever eager for connections in high places, Peter had befriended the judge's wayward son. A year later, Peter would learn of Amos Mushili's tragic encounter with a woman of the night and his conviction and subsequent sentencing to prison for manslaughter. Little did Peter know at the time that he would one day need the services of his ignominious friend in a sensitive matter of British Intelligence.

Henry Hinckley had been recruited by MI6, Britain's foreign intelligence wing, back in London in 1955. Following his training in covert operations, which even his famous uncle Rab Butler was unaware of, he had been sent to Northern Rhodesia. His express mission was to gather actionable intelligence that could be used by the British government to dismantle the African independence movement which was rapidly gaining momentum. At the time, British colonies all over central Africa were grappling with increasingly violent attacks born of unrest in the indigenous African population over colonial rule. Henry was sent under the guise of a mineral prospector working for a renowned company called Chesterman and Oakley. Ultimately, the British government's efforts to thwart the freedom struggle proved unsuccessful and the indigenous Africans in Northern Rhodesia were able to gain their independence from Britain in '64. Britain was now faced with two options for what to do with their numerous intelligence operatives stationed in the new independent country of Zambia: recall them to Britain to be redeployed elsewhere or keep them in place but with a new charter. Britain chose to keep many of its intelligence officers in place so as to maintain its influence on the new mineral rich republic. Henry was one of those officers.

Somewhere along the way Henry Hinckley went rogue. The British government became aware of his trafficking in illicit precious stones and they threatened to recall him to face punishment in Britain. The prospect of spending the rest of his life in a British prison had led Henry to snap. A covert intelligence officer with his level of experience knew many secrets, things that could prove harmful to the British government. Henry threatened to make public a list he had gathered over the years of names and addresses of fellow covert operatives across Africa, if MI6 didn't leave him alone. He had gone too far and his gamble would ultimately prove to be his demise.

MI6 began to monitor Henry's every move. They tapped his telephone and placed recording devices in his car and in his home. They followed and listened in to conversations with all his friends, business partners and acquaintances. They were fully aware of his long-time friend Frits Hubercht's financial woes and Henry's intentions of helping him. When Henry suddenly suffered a debilitating stroke, MI6 breathed a collective sigh of relief but they needed to get a hold of the list which he claimed to have generated. They could not risk other operatives in the field being exposed or compromised. Then another stroke of luck. From a conversation Peter James had with his erstwhile acquaintance Amos Mushili, who had recently been released from prison, and loquacious with alcohol, he gleaned that a scheme was afoot to stage a break-in at Hinckley Farm that was being orchestrated by a friend of the Hinckleys. It was an opportunity too good to pass up. Peter, young and arrogant, easily shrugged off the possibility that the two old people might be hurt. The means justified the end. His self-satisfied smile was a cruel one.

Amos Mushili had at first been disinterested in Paul Mutamina's proposition to help him break into a *muzungu* couple's farmhouse way out in rural Makeni. What valuables could they possibly have that would make it worth his while? He declined to do it. However, after talking with Peter James at the poolside of Pamodzi Hotel, Amos was convinced otherwise. The white man had proposed a deal that had widened his opportunistic eyes. Peter had told him that the British government had been monitoring the Hinckleys for several months and they had confirmed that they were engaged in trafficking of emeralds. In fact, they were certain that there were some hidden in the Hinckley farmhouse. From their estimation, it could fetch a very handsome sum on the black market; moreover it was ill-gotten contraband meaning that only the Hinckley's would miss them; they would not even be able to report the theft to the police. Peter explained that he was not interested in the gemstones, all he needed was a list of names which he knew was hidden somewhere in the house. "Bring me the list and you can keep the stones and whatever else of value you find." He had said.

After sharing a few drinks, the two men walked through a short corridor which opened up into a foyer. They stood a few feet apart facing each other underneath an ornate chandelier. "So thanks to you, I can now walk freely again." Amos said.

Peter nodded. "The investigation has ceased, suspects have been apprehended and they've confessed to the crime. They'll be swiftly tried … It is, as they say, an open and shut case." He then paused. He extended a hand to Amos. "Well, I needn't say more. My only advice to you would be to keep a low profile for now, there's no use in rubbing their noses in it, at least until it's been through the courts."

They shook hands and parted ways with a vague promise to see each other again under more convivial circumstances.

The night watchman closed the metal gate behind Amos. He heard the clanging of metal as the guard secured the padlock. The street was empty at this time of night. A row of street lamps provided dim lighting on one side of the street. Amos placed a cap over his head and pulled the zipper on his bomber jacket up to his chin. Placing his hands inside his pockets, he crossed to the darker side of the street. It was safer to walk in the shadows for he knew that police officers sometimes patrolled the rich neighbourhoods in a bid to catch loiterers and would be burglars, it was called *shishita*.

It was a cool night with a sharp breeze. He walked briskly down towards the mouth of the cul-de-sac. He soon reached the corner where he noticed a white Fiat GLS parked on the far side of the adjoining street. It was too dark and too far to tell if there was anyone inside it.

Almost an hour later Amos found himself inside a back alley bar in Bauleni compound. There was certainly cause for celebration, he had escaped with the skin of his teeth and he knew it. The weight of the small parcel of emeralds in his pocket made him smile. He needed a couple more drinks before turning it in for the night. Bars in Bauleni were not quite up to his usual standards but a drink was a drink and he knew he still had to keep a low profile.

Several drinks later, Amos was feeling very light-headed, as he made his way through a maze of narrow footpaths until he was back again onto the main tarred road which he had used earlier. He was but a fifteen minute walk along the main road to where he had rented a motel room for the night. The street was empty, most of the city asleep. Then suddenly the headlights of a car appeared ahead of him. The vehicle swerved towards him. Amos jumped, the car grazing him in the left leg. It stopped several metres away and began to turn. He'd been double-crossed by Peter James ... Birds of a feather, he should have known he'd never be safe ...

❋

11:48 a.m.

Day of Queen Elizabeth's arrival

University Teaching Hospital, Nationalist Road, Lusaka

It took Maxwell much longer than it would ordinarily have taken him to reach the University Teaching Hospital from the Central Police Station on account of the roads blocked off for security during the Queen's arrival. When he finally arrived, he was met by two junior officers who took him directly to the mortuary. One of the officers explained to Max that they had cause to believe that a body of a man that had been found on the side of a road near Bauleni compound was that of the notorious Amos Kapambewe Mushili. The young officer described how they had been called in the early hours of Thursday morning to attend to a suspected hit and run case. "It must have occurred very late at night, there were no witnesses and nobody saw anything." He said adjusting his hat. He went on to tell Max that when he saw the body he was sure he had seen the face before, it took him a little while but he remembered the picture of the fugitive Amos Mushili that had been circulated in the police station several days earlier.

"Did they find anything on him? Identification papers? Contraband? Anything at all?" Maxwell asked.

The officer nodded. "He had a stolen driver's permit for Southern Rhodesia. I remembered that too … the alert in the station that Mushili was probably traveling under an alias."

"There was nothing else found on him?"

"No *sah*, just the papers and some cash *sah* … he had been drinking in Bauleni, a few people we spoke with remembered seeing him. They said he was alone."

Max rubbed his chin. He had to see the body for himself.

They entered the frigid room where bodies were kept in state waiting for loved ones to claim them. After a short conversation and a check against handwritten entries in a thick logbook, a slow hefty man in green uniform led them to a metallic shelf with a string of covered bodies. Max found it hard to breathe, the place smelled of death, a morbid reminder of everyone's ultimate fate. When the plastic cover was peeled back, Max stared at the body lying lifeless in front of him. There was no mistaking it, indeed it was Amos Mushili.

Max stepped into the fresh air outside the building and made his way past the verandah to stand underneath the shade of a tree. He pulled out a cigarette and lit it. Pulling on the stick he reflected on the whirlwind of events over the past several days. So much blood, so many lives lost, their families left to pick up the pieces and all for what? Amos Mushili was no more, he would no longer be able to hurt or kill anyone else but somehow a bitter taste was left in Maxwell's mouth. He would have to interview the people who had last seen Amos but inside he knew it would probably lead to a dead end and it was impossible to know where or who was now in possession of the emeralds. He peered into the distance where he saw a nurse assisting an elderly man with a cane entering the building. Max blew smoke into the air above him. He was still a believer in the existence of good in the world and that bad people often get what is coming to them. Indeed, it would seem that in this instance, fate had delivered its own disquieting form of justice.

Acknowledgements

This project was by no means a solitary pursuit. In the almost two year process of writing this novel, I benefited from the help of a great number of people. I will do my best to acknowledge many of those who contributed to making this book a reality. If my words fail me, please blame it on the inadequacies of my head and not my heart.

To my mother who was always an ardent supporter of my writing, thank you for everything. I'm sad that you did not live to see this book published but I know you are watching down on me. To my wife, Sandra, you have been an unwavering companion on this literary journey. Thank you for your encouragement, your understanding and for frequently creating the quiet time for me to write. I am also grateful for all of your unheralded work in creating the 'author brand'. We are truly equal partners in this endeavour.

My dearest Malaika, you bring me immeasurable joy every day. I especially enjoy our moments together when we sit down to read. Papa loves you and I hope that one day you will enjoy reading my stories.

To Dad, you are the epitome of what it means to be a good and decent man. You face every challenge in life with dignity and poise. Thank you for your love and support. Your feedback on my work has been invaluable. To my siblings, Mwewa, Saka and Kanyanta, thank you for reading early drafts of my work and for your enthusiastic support for my writing.

As is the case with every African on the face of this earth, I have an expansive extended family. I cannot mention each one of you here by name for that would be the length of yet another novel. My sincere gratitude to all of you, I am because you are - Ubuntu.

To my publisher, Weaver Press, thank you for believing in this story. It has been yet another tremendous journey. I love the creative process. You have been beacons of great African literature for so many years.

Gadsden Publishers, you led the way in supporting Zambian writers. I am grateful for all that you do. Keep the fire burning, we need to tell our own stories.

I would also like to thank the University of Zambia, Mulungushi University, University of Witwatersrand, and all the other institutions of learning that have supported my work.

Lastly, but in no way the least, I want to thank all of my readers and followers on my website (www.mukukachipanta.com), Facebook (@chipantamukuka), Instagram (mukukachipanta), Twitter (@Chipanta), on blogs as well as on podcast platforms (Apple Podcasts, iTunes, Stitcher and Google Music Play). It always amazes me when people write to tell me about their depth of feeling for plot lines and characters that I created in the stillness of my thoughts - indeed there is no greater accolade.

Printed in the United States
By Bookmasters